Rebecca Barrett

Callahan
and the
Spy

Secret Staircase Books

REBECCA BARRETT

Callahan and the Spy

Callahan and the Spy
Published by Secret Staircase Books, an imprint of
Columbine Publishing Group LLC
PO Box 416, Angel Fire, NM 87710

Book layout and design by Secret Staircase Books
Illustrations by Becky's Graphic Design, Oxilixo, Svetlana
Dubovetcaia, Irina88w, Lenanet, Cammeraydave, Dmitry Kotin
First e-book edition: June, 2024
First paperback edition: June, 2024

Publisher's Cataloging-in-Publication Data

Barrett, Rebecca
Callahan and the Spy / by Rebecca Barrett.
p. cm.
ISBN 978-1649141798 (paperback)
ISBN 978-1649141804 (e-book)

1. Cat Callahan (Fictitious character)—Fiction. 2. Mystery—
Fiction. 3. Amateur sleuths—Fiction. 4. Animals in mystery fiction.
I. Title

Cat Callahan Mystery Series, Book 5.
Barrett, Rebecca, Cat Callahan Cozy Mysteries.

BISAC : FICTION / Mystery.

813/.54

For Ginger McSween, the original Ginger, minus the Titian hair. Steadfast friend, animal lover, and champion of lost causes.

Chapter One

*H*ello, Trout," *Ginger says.*

Instantly I rise from a light snooze on the window seat overlooking Petronia Street. Unfortunately, the greeting isn't for the vision of trout almandine already forming in my feline mind. It is, instead, addressed to a sandy haired man in deck shoes, tattered khaki shorts, and a faded Hawaiian print shirt standing in the center of the foyer.

"Ginger." *The man called Trout says.*

"What brings you to the Paradise?"

"My morning charter. She was supposed to be at the marina at six."

"One of mine?"

"Yeah."

"Name?"

"Liberty Anderson."

"That would be the Toucan Suite. Not exactly your usual fare."

Trout shrugged. "Her money spends like any other."

Trout exudes an intoxicating mixture of scents: sea air, cotton dried in the sun, fish. I admit the latter is enough to draw me to examine his deck shoes.

"I see one of the Hemingway cats has strayed from home again." *He places his hands in the pockets of his shorts and watches me as I investigate.*

"He's not a museum cat." *Ginger replies.*

"Yours? You've gotten yourself a pet?"

"He belongs to a guy named Dax. He's doing some work for me. Converting the garage into an apartment. And some other odds and ends I've let slide for too long."

Trout loses interest in me and crosses to the reception desk. He places an elbow on the high mahogany counter and runs his other hand through overlong, curling hair, and sighs. "You want to hustle up my charter?"

"Sure." *Ginger picks up the phone receiver and punches in two numbers. She watches Trout as she listens to the barely audible burring ring of the phone in the Toucan Suite drifting down the stairwell to the reception area. After several rings, she lets the receiver fall away from her ear and dangle from her curled fingers. She raises her eyebrows.* "Did you try her cell phone?"

"For the past forty-five minutes. I decided the battery must be dead." *He rubs the stubble on his chin.* "You haven't seen her this morning, have you?"

Ginger hangs up the phone and shakes her head. "I've been up and busy with breakfast since five. She could have slipped out for a run while I was in the kitchen." *She glances at the line of hooks on the wall behind the reception desk.* "Her key's not here, so probably not." *She hesitates then says,* "Coffee's on. You look like you could use a cup."

Ah, what's this? Do I detect a hint of interest on the part of Ginger? There's something in her voice that makes me wonder, a very subtle something, but it's there, nevertheless. I turn my attention once again to Trout. What is it about this particular male that strikes a chord with the world-weary mistress of the Paradise Bed and Breakfast?

"Do you think you could check to see if she's in her room?" *he asks.*

Ginger leans back from the reception counter. "I don't normally like to disturb my guests unless they request a wake-up call, but sure." *The something has disappeared from her voice. She takes the ring of master keys from a drawer.*

"Thanks." *Trout jangles the change in his pocket.* "I was counting on the booking. I'm a little pinched right now."

The faint lines on Ginger's forehead smooth and she crosses the foyer to the stairs. I decide this is my opportunity to explore the Toucan Suite. The guest who booked it has been very standoffish and doesn't appear to have much affection for cats, and me, in particular. She's been quick to close her door on my inquisitive nose. She even had the nerve to tell me to "scat." *Now I'm on a mission to gain access to her room just for the heck of it. After all, she brought it upon herself.*

Ginger knocks on the door of the Toucan Suite and waits, keys in hand. She glances down at me, arches an eyebrow and says, "Behave."

What? Dax and I have only been in town three days. Why would she think I wouldn't behave?

The knock goes unanswered and Ginger frowns. She knocks harder and when there is still no answer, no sound of anyone stirring within the suite, she sighs.

I can see that she's hesitant to intrude on the privacy of a guest at this early hour, but it appears the desire to accommodate Trout overcomes her misgivings. She uses the master key and opens the door.

Sprawled across the bed is the guest I have labeled Birdbrain. I instantly catch a whiff of an unusual scent, one I haven't yet encountered in my ramblings. Underlying that rapidly fading odor is one that is all too familiar. Liberty Anderson will never again shoo cats or any other creatures from her door. She is dead in Paradise.

Ginger hesitates on the threshold as if she too senses the absence of life in the pale body before her. She clears her throat. "Ms. Anderson."

I pad across the room to the foot of the bed where one hand trails to the floor. "Yeow." I sit and blink at Ginger.

"Liberty?" *This time Ginger speaks louder and takes a couple of steps into the room.* "Liberty Anderson!"

She moves quickly to the side of the woman in red sprawled across the still-made bed and now sees the already clouding blue eyes open in an expression of what could be considered astonishment.

Ginger places two fingers against the artery in the woman's neck for a couple of seconds then backs away to the door. "Trout!" *she calls down the stairs.* "You'd better get up here."

* * *

Ginger's heart tapped a double beat when she looked down into the lifeless eyes of the woman in the Toucan Suite. She knew Liberty Anderson was dead even before she checked for a pulse.

Her mind raced ahead with questions she knew the police would ask the moment they arrived. Ginger needed to call them right away, but she couldn't seem to move. Her gaze followed the movements of the funny-looking gray cat called Callahan. He sniffed the dead woman's hand then leapt onto the bed and sniffed around her mouth.

Was this what had set the cat off in the middle of the night? Ginger thought back to the images of his meltdown at one in the morning. He had demanded to be admitted to the bed and breakfast with his caterwauling. But Liberty hadn't been in her room then. The keys to her suite had been on the board behind the registration desk.

She took a deep breath and released it slowly. Trout topped the stairs and came to stand beside her, looking into the room.

"Passed out?" he asked.

"Dead," she replied.

* * *

Trout looked from the dead woman to Ginger, then back again. He didn't need to enter the room to know that Ginger was right in her assessment of the situation. There's a stillness in death that's like no other and, with the exception of the dumpy gray cat with the golden eyes, there was no life emanating from the room.

He shifted his body weight away from the doorway, an involuntary movement brought on by other deaths and other lonely hotel rooms.

The police would need to be called and the process of a suspicious death would begin. He didn't plan to stick around for the formalities.

He jangled the change in his pocket. "Was she ill, do you know? A heart condition or something?"

"I've no idea. She's just a tourist doing the tourist thing."

"The tourist thing?"

"Sleeping late, out half the night, dressed for…" Ginger hesitated. The woman was dead, for Pete's sake.

"Action?" Trout suggested.

"She was having a good time. Let's just leave it at that."

"Did she bring anyone back to the Paradise?"

"No."

"All right, then. I guess we should call nine-one-one." He watched as the cat worked his way down the length of Liberty Anderson's body, sniffing the whole way. "And get that damn cat away from her." The cat paused at the woman's left foot and fixated on her big toe then lost interest.

Unwilling to break the plane of the door casing, Trout made a hissing sound through his teeth in an effort to scare the cat off the bed. The cat flattened his already floppy ears and sniffed one last time. He then sat back on his haunches and observed Trout through the narrow slits of his golden eyes.

Ginger gave a small shake of her head and sighed. "Callahan," she said, "off the bed."

The cat called Callahan turned his gaze to Ginger, blinked three times, and hopped down from the bed. He made his way silently to the purse and its spilled contents on the floor by the dressing table. After he examined all the items, he padded off into the bathroom.

"Crazy cat," Trout said. Neither he nor Ginger made a move to set in motion what they both knew had to happen. It occurred to Trout that a dead body at the bed and breakfast couldn't be good for Ginger's business. Late summer wasn't the most lucrative time of the year for either of them. Fewer tourists were willing to risk a ruined vacation at the height of hurricane season. Parents were getting children ready to return to school, and retirees didn't want to be in the sub-tropics when temperatures ranged in the high nineties and the humidity was off the charts.

It was as if the inability to rally to action lifted from each of them at the same time. Trout and Ginger turned toward the head of the stairs.

When they reached the ground floor, Trout looked at Ginger. "You okay?"

She nodded.

He noted the paleness around her lips. He had hoped to skip out while she phoned the police. He didn't want to get tangled up with an investigation. After all, he didn't know the dead woman. Not really. She was simply a charter to him.

When Ginger reached for the phone on the reception desk, he noted the slight tremble of her hand. He had left it too late. His window of opportunity slammed shut. He couldn't leave her now that he knew how shaken she was.

He had known Ginger since he first landed in Key West almost two years ago. After a six-month hiatus he thought of as his lost period, he had looked around for a means to support himself. He crewed on a couple of deep-sea fishing boats for the remainder of that year and decided this was the life for him.

During that first year, he had seen Ginger on occasion at the Smokin' Tuna, a restaurant and bar frequented in the after-hours, off-season, by locals. She, and a couple of other small establishments had been willing to keep fliers of his charter company available for interested guests.

When he was near the end of a six-pack, Trout acknowledged to himself that he was more than a little attracted to her. In his more sober moments, he never allowed his thoughts to linger in such treacherous waters. Trout had purposely chosen the life of a loner and Key West was an ideal setting for like-minded people.

The gray cat caught Trout's eye as he came down the stairs. He paused on the third step from the bottom and sat, curling his tail around his front paws. Trout was accustomed to the Hemingway cats that roamed the island as well as the conchs who made Key West their home. This cat, Callahan, Ginger had called him, wasn't like any of them. He had strange ears that didn't stand up straight and he had a less than sleek body. In fact, he was more than a little dumpy.

Trout listened to Ginger's end of the phone conversation with the police. They had her stay on the line, so he went through to the kitchen and poured each of them a cup of coffee. He hesitated over the blueberry muffins but decided it would be unseemly to take one under the circumstances.

* * *

Ginger accepted the steaming cup of coffee from Trout with a nod of thanks. She had hung up on the nine-one-one operator after assuring her that she wasn't in any danger, there was nothing anyone could do for the woman in the Toucan Suite, and that she wasn't going anywhere.

As she sipped the hot brew, she realized her hands were no longer shaking and her mind was reviewing the details of the room when she had first opened the door to the Toucan Suite. The image that stuck in her mind was the lone red shoe that rested on its side on the floor just below where Liberty Anderson's left foot rested half on and half off the bed.

"Is this your first dead body?" Trout asked.

Ginger cleared her throat, but in the end only shook her head.

The sound of a police siren grew louder as it approached from the direction of Truman Avenue. She took another sip of coffee and placed the cup on the registration counter.

"Did you smell anything in the room?" she asked Trout.

He thought for a second, his forehead creased with a frown, and shook his head. "No." He looked down at Ginger. "Like perfume you mean?"

"Not that exactly." She glanced toward the front door where two uniformed police officers were entering the building. "It was an unusual scent, very faint." Her shoulders lifted in a slight shrug. "Probably just my imagination."

Ginger knew Trout didn't want to be there, that the thought of becoming entangled in the investigation had him halfway to the door. She was grateful that he had remained with her, had given her time to recover from the initial shock of her discovery. "Sorry about all this," she said.

Trout jangled his change once again. "What are friends for, right?"

Friends. They were friends. She had felt drawn to him the first time she saw him balancing precariously on a bar stool at the Bull and Whistle, his head in his hand. His hollowed-out eyes and morning shakes had, with time, given way to a permanent tan that made his pale blue eyes startling when you first saw him. His frame had filled out with hard work and the slow return of his appetite.

Whatever had driven him to abandon his former life

and bury himself in the Florida Keys was still a mystery to her. It was a common state of being for many who drifted down the state seeking some intangible something. Or seeking nothing at all.

Ginger didn't know which it was with Trout.

One of the police officers went up the stairs to stand guard over the body in the Toucan Suite while the other separated her and Trout. She saw Trout's wistful glance at the front entrance of the Paradise as the policeman motioned for him to wait in the kitchen. A twinge of guilt tugged at her. She should have sent him on his way the moment she got off the phone with the police. Now it was too late.

Duncan Moore strolled through the beveled glass front doors of the Paradise. One of the uniformed policemen intercepted him, obviously giving him the run-down on the situation.

Of all the people they could have sent, Ginger thought. She had mentally prepared herself for Ricki Lofton, a detective with the police force and a friend. Instead, she had Duncan.

"Ginger." Duncan shrugged his shoulders in that forward roll of his. "Got a bit of a complication, I hear."

Duncan and Ginger had fallen into a short-lived relationship a couple of years back when she first returned to Key West to take over the Paradise. He was a handsome man with his dark hair beginning to gray at the temples, deep blue eyes, and a compact but solid physique. The problem with Duncan was he had a habit of falling into short-lived relationships.

Ginger had long since gotten over Duncan. In truth, she had known, going in, the kind of man he was. Their relationship had been more about lust than love. She had known that going in, too. At the time, they had met a need for each other. His presence on the case as the detective wasn't ideal.

"Duncan. How've you been?"

"Same old, same old."

The humor in the situation struck Ginger and she laughed. "I don't doubt that one bit, Duncan. Not one bit."

He grinned. "You know me, Ginger. I get restless."

"Who's on the line now?"

He shrugged again. "Free floating at the moment."

"When aren't you free floating?"

"You're looking good."

"If forty looks good on anyone."

"You know what they say. Forty is the new thirty."

"I'm a long way from thirty."

"Yeah, but you're not forty either. More like thirty-five, right?"

"Close enough."

"Whatever. You look damn good. Things seem to be going well for you."

"If you don't consider the dead body in my most expensive suite."

"Yeah. About that. Who is she?"

"Liberty Anderson. She checked in four days ago."

"You found her in her room dead?"

"Yes."

"Door locked?"

"Yes."

"Help me out here, Ginger." A note of exasperation underlined his words.

Ginger crossed her arms at waist level. "I don't know

when she came in last night. She wasn't in her room at one."

"And how do you know that?"

"The cat started yowling."

"Cat? You got a cat?"

"No. He belongs to a friend."

As if on cue, Callahan sauntered into the reception area from the direction of the kitchen. He gave Duncan an assessing up and down and continued on to the stairs.

"A friend, huh?"

"Do you want to hear the rest of the story?"

"Sure, sure."

"Ms. Anderson didn't like cats."

"Imagine that."

"So, I came to see what had set him off. I didn't want him disturbing the guests."

"What set him off?"

"I don't know. I opened the front door and he raced up the stairs. He wanted to get into Ms. Anderson's room. He kept pacing outside the door then he would stop and reach his paw up to the doorknob. Bat at it."

"You let him in?"

"Of course not. I picked him up and took him to my room."

"So how did you know she wasn't in for the night?"

"The key. I use the big old-fashioned keys for the rooms so people don't walk off with them."

"I remember."

Ginger frowned. "Anyway, her key was still on the hook."

"Was it there when you first turned in?"

Ginger stared at the row of hooks and keys on a board

behind the reception desk trying to evoke the image of it as it was when she made her rounds before bedtime. She couldn't be sure. "I don't know."

Duncan watched the cat sitting on the third stairstep. "What made you check her room this morning?"

When she didn't respond immediately, Duncan forgot about the cat and looked at Ginger. She glanced away from his scrutiny and down at the floor.

"Trout," she said.

"Trout?"

Ginger squared her shoulders and looked into Duncan's eyes. She could almost see him searching through all the facts and detritus that is the mind of a cop. "He bought Big Mouth's rig last year."

Duncan nodded absently, his mental process finally settling on a memory. "The guy in the kitchen." He thought for a moment. "What did he have to do with it?"

"She was a charter for this morning. When she didn't show up, he came looking for her."

"Why would he do that? Why not just charge her for the missed charter?"

"He's not like that?"

"Like what? A good businessman?"

"He wouldn't just take her money."

Duncan watched her, a look of speculation in his eyes. "So, he came looking for her."

Ginger nodded. "I called the room and got no answer." She hesitated. "Then I decided to check her room."

"You said the door was locked."

"Yes. I used my pass key." Ginger looked away from Duncan's probing regard. "There she was, lying across the bed, fully clothed. Except for the shoe."

"The shoe?"

"Yes. The left shoe had fallen off. It was on the floor."

"How did you know she was dead?"

"I didn't at first but when she didn't respond when I called her name," Ginger gave her head a small shake, "she was just so still. Too still. I just knew."

"Did you enter the room?"

She nodded. "I checked her pulse at her throat, but I already knew. The eyes..." she looked away again.

"Yeah." Duncan was silent for a moment. "Did you touch anything?"

"No."

"How about the boat captain?"

"He never entered the room."

"Okay." He touched her lightly on the upper arm, not quite a pat but only long enough to offer reassurance. "She might have been diabetic or had a heart condition or something. Let's not read anything into it."

"But she's so young. She looks to be in her late twenties."

"Yeah, well don't worry, okay? Old age isn't the only cause of death. The coroner will figure it out."

Ginger nodded.

"Who else was working last night?"

"No one. Jules works every other night for me to man the desk and phone. If a guest needs something, whoever has the shift takes care of it. There's a daybed in the little office behind the desk." She indicated the door behind her with a jerk of her head. "Last night was my night on duty. I sleep in my room but have a monitor so I can hear what's going on in the foyer."

"Like a baby monitor?"

She nodded.

"And you didn't hear her come in last night?"

"No."

"Any other staff on the premises?"

Ginger shook her head. "The bar closes at eleven, so Harry left about eleven-fifteen, eleven-twenty. Angela doesn't come in until seven each morning. I start the coffee and do the set up for breakfast. She comes in to start serving. Afterward, she helps with the cleaning until noon. When she got here this morning, the first policemen on the scene had just arrived. They sent her home."

"That's your whole staff?"

"Yes. Four people. I only serve breakfast and then finger sandwiches at tea. If anyone gets hungry at night, there's a food station in the butler's pantry. They can get a soft drink, water, cookies. Things like that."

"That's a lean operation."

"What can I say? It's what I can afford. Besides, with the two cottages that's only seven rooms."

"How many guests are registered right now?"

"Four rooms. A total of six guests. Well, except for Liberty, that makes five, I guess."

"I'll want their names. Save me the trouble later if there's anything to be concerned about."

"Sure." Ginger went behind the reception desk and booted up the computer. With a few keystrokes, she printed out a list for Duncan.

He scanned down the list, folded it, and put it in his inside coat pocket as he turned toward the kitchen.

"Don't you want to see the body?"

He glanced back at Ginger. "In due course."

Chapter Two

Trout washed down the last of the blueberry muffin with the dregs in his coffee cup as the kitchen door swung open.

He recognized the man who sauntered into the kitchen and gave him the once over. He had seen him here and there around Key West, mainly at the Smokin' Tuna. At the time, Trout had figured him for a cop. There was something about the body language that was universal.

"Trout," the man said. "Is that some kind of nickname?"

Trout nodded. "Armentrout. Richardson."

The cop whistled softly. "That's some moniker. Your folks must have really loved you."

Trout made no reply. He didn't plan on being drawn into a play at being best buds in a relationship he knew could only end as adversarial.

The cop let the silence draw out. He went to the coffee maker and poured himself a cup. After a tentative sip he said, "You found the body?"

"No." Trout waited until the detective looked up at him. "Ginger found her."

"I hear you're a very conscientious kind of guy."

"How's that?"

"You always go in search of fares that don't show up?"

"Not always."

"Just this time."

Trout said nothing.

"How well did you know Ms. Anderson?"

"Not at all. Not really."

"Which is it? Not at all or not really?"

Trout sighed and shook his head. "I saw her last night, but I didn't know she was my charter until this morning. When we found her."

The detective did a shoulder roll then caught a thumb in the waistband of his slacks. "By *saw her*, you mean what? Exactly."

"She was at the Bull and Whistle. At the bar making friends with anyone and everyone."

"And you noticed her particularly because?"

"The red dress. The whole Marilyn Monroe look she had going on."

"But you didn't know who she was."

"She said her name was Alice."

The detective watched Trout a moment longer then took another sip of his coffee. "So, you didn't just see her, you spoke to her. What else did you do if I might be so bold as to ask."

"Nothing."

"You didn't buy her drinks? Take a spin on the dance floor? Show her the sights of Key West?"

Trout tamped down his rising anger at the detective's tone. This was exactly what he knew would happen if he got sucked into this investigation. Once again, his motives would be called into question. "Look. I was sitting at the bar, she came in and sat next to me, and we chatted. She wanted to know where the Oriole was. Said her taxi driver told her about it and she was all fired up to experience the real night life of Key West."

"And the two of you trundled along to the Oriole."

"No. I finished my drink and headed back to the boat. I had an early charter."

"And you didn't know it was with the woman at the bar?"

"Like I said."

"Why would she say her name was Alice?"

"Can't help you there. Maybe she was doing the Vegas thing."

"What Vegas thing?"

"You know. What happens in Vegas stays in Vegas."

"Huh." The detective drained his cup of coffee and eyed the blueberry muffins. "Strange coincidence, wouldn't you say?"

"What's that?"

"That you should run into a woman you didn't know, with whom you had an early morning charter, on the very night before she's found dead in her room."

"Key West is a small place."

"Not that small."

* * *

People like me, generally speaking. Just ask Lil the Librarian back in Warm Springs. Her door was never closed to me. Well, the door of the library, anyway. There was always something tasty for a snack and a good gossip about what was going on around town. This Detective Moore, however, is unimpressed by my Scottish ears and my cuddly appearance. In fact, I'd guess he's taken a dislike to me.

One of his policemen has grabbed me and dumped me into Ginger's arms with the stern order to keep me from underfoot. He doesn't appreciate the fact that I'm his best bet to solve this case. Call it curiosity, call it my keen senses, call it superior intelligence. You can call me anything but don't call me late to supper. Sorry. Couldn't help myself.

But Dax doesn't call me Dirty Harry for nothing.

Moore's attitude toward me isn't important. It's the less-than-thorough approach to the circumstances of this case that worries me. To the police, Liberty Anderson's death is a mystery but not yet a crime. I can only hope the coroner is more aware.

I regret my behavior last night. It was a childish prank, I confess, to gain access to the bed and breakfast. But, in my defense, I was hungry and at loose ends. I don't know where Dax had wandered off to after work but wherever it was, it didn't look like he'd be returning any time soon. In case you didn't know, I'm not good with time. A minute, an hour, they're pretty much the same to me. So, let's call it hunger and boredom and be done with it.

And, the temper tantrum outside the Birdbrain's door, now that was childish, too. If I had only known she was in danger. But how could I? There was no hint of it at the time, no telltale scent lingering in the air. I guess I was just in a mood to vent, as the humans say. The inscrutable behavior of a cat. But since no one's asking, it doesn't really matter anyway. Certainly not the cop who's eyeing Trout with a look I recognize.

With a grunt, the policeman sends Trout on his way with a

relieved expression on his face. I find I can tolerate Trout's company. He did understand that I was about to faint from hunger while he waited to be interviewed by Moore. He gave me not one, but two of Ginger's blueberry muffins. A dollop of cream would have been appreciated but it's early days yet. I should be able to whip him into shape quickly. After all, the work on the new garage apartment of the Paradise will easily take Dax a couple of weeks, if not more. I won't mind that much. Key West is a laid back kind of place. There are cats everywhere. And chickens. I'm sure there's a story behind that.

A piece of yellow tape has been placed across the casing of the closed Toucan Suite door. Ginger is distracted, and perhaps a bit distressed, by the demands from two of her guests to be checked out of their rooms immediately. The fact that they will have to remain in Key West until the police determine the cause of death has them in a hostile mood. Not even the fact that their reservations would have kept them in town for three more nights seems to bear weight with them.

It appears it will be up to me to find out what really happened to Liberty Anderson and restore Ginger's business. For a moment I had hopes that Trout would jump into the fray. There is chemistry between those two. I can tell. Needless to say, I've spent a lifetime studying humans. Perhaps he'll come around.

In the meantime, I'll check out the area, learn the lay of the land, see how someone could have gained access to the locked Toucan Suite because I'm certain the murderer laid in wait for his victim. Access, that's the tricky question, but I'll find the answer. And, yes, I did say murderer. I'm sure of it. Well, I'm pretty sure.

I slip out through the front door of the Paradise on the heels of a policeman. The grounds of the bed and breakfast are lush with foliage, and I'm briefly distracted by a rather large iguana. He must be at least two and a half feet long, tail to nose. We engage in a

Mexican stand-off, his beady eyes unflinching, but one flick of my tail and he darts away.

At the rear of the house is a narrow back porch that runs the length of the building. On the southeast corner a staircase runs up the east side to the second floor. At the top of these stairs, lying on his back, sprawled across the landing, is a very fat, pale gray cat. Beside him is a petite gray with white markings.

As I top the stairs the petite gray ceases her complaining and turns her cross-eyed gaze on me. Obviously curious about the cause of the sudden silence, the fat cat opens his eyes.

"Who're you?" he asks.

"Callahan."

He wriggles and squirms until he can get his feet under him, and he strolls over to me. "What kind of name is that? Callahan?"

I suppress a sigh. "It's a human name."

The female begins to purr, moves beside the fat cat, and touches her nose to mine. Her eyes are very disconcerting.

"I'm Megs," *she says.*

The fat cat muscles her to the side. "Where'd you come from?"

"Warm Springs. Sort of."

"What's that? An ocean?"

"A city."

"Oh."

They stare at me as if I had said the moon.

I know Ginger doesn't own any pets. "Where'd you come from?"

The female motions with her head toward the east. "The museum. We're Hemingway cats."

The tone of her voice suggests I should be impressed by this revelation. When she gets no reaction from me, she holds up her paw, revealing five toes spread apart as if this is something special. At my lack of response, she glances at the fat cat, and says, "Show him, Bartholomew."

Bartholomew grunts and lies back down, ignoring me and Megs.

She sidles up to me and rubs along the length of my body, purring all the while. "So, what brings you to Key West?"

I confess, vanity made me say it. And annoyance at Bartholomew's attitude. "Murder."

Bartholomew lifts his large head, opens his eyes, and stares at me. Megs does a funny little quick step, right paw over left paw, left paw over right, three times in rapid succession.

Still unimpressed Bartholomew says, "Who'd you kill, a mouse?" *Then he grins.*

That rather deflates my ego. "No one," *I say,* "I'm a detective."

"Wow." *Megs moves right up in my face.* "You mean you solve crimes? Catch murderers?"

"Exactly."

Bartholomew grunts, lies his head down, closes his eyes, and rolls onto his back.

"Are you on a case? Are you on a case?" *Megs does her little dance.*

Normally I play my cards close to my chest but given that Megs and Bartholomew appear to use the premises as they please, I can see the benefit of putting them in the know.

"Where were you both last night?"

"You are on a case!" *Meg's crossed-eyes almost twirl like a whirly-gig in her excitement.* "Is it murder?"

"Yes, I'm on a case and it's most definitely murder."

"Oh, oh, oh! Can I help? Can I be your sidekick?"

"What you can do is tell me if you were on the grounds of the Paradise last night and anything you saw."

"Yes!" *Megs does her little dance.* "We were a…"

"Megs!" *Bartholomew growls and rocks back and forth until his great weight shifts and he is once again on his feet.* "We were at the museum, in our beds in the cat house. We weren't spying on anyone."

"Oh, right." *Megs says as she looks from me to Bartholomew then back to me.* "We weren't violating the court order. Honest."

"What court order?"

Bartholomew yawns. "What are you talking about?" *he asks.* "We're cats. We know nothing of legal wranglings and officious secret agents." *He suddenly discovers a need to groom between his many toes.*

Megs lowers her eyes and moves to the corner of the landing, gazing out across the back lawn. She won't look at me.

Well, something is afoot here, but it'll have to take a back seat to the matter at hand. Whatever these two know could be vital to finding a killer.

* * *

Ginger balanced the stack of clean linens on her hip as she fished in her pocket for the key to the newly vacated Flamingo Suite. It was the middle room of three on the front of the Paradise and one of the most expensive because of the gallery access. The loss of three nights occupancy would hurt. She could only hope the Williamsons would decide not to do a review on any of the travel websites.

Just as she inserted the key in the lock, she heard the muffled tones of a ringing cell phone. It was coming from the Toucan Suite next door.

She placed the linens on a hallway table and held her ear to the door, listening. The phone continued to ring insistently. She stepped back and eyed the crime scene tape along the door casing.

"Crap." With the key she sliced through the tape and entered the room. As soon as she stepped over the threshold the phone stopped ringing but not before Ginger had an idea of where the sound came from.

She had already violated Duncan's instructions that no one enter the room so she might as well go all in and find the phone. The dying ring had come from the area of the dressing table.

The police had taken all of Liberty's beauty aids from it. All that remained was a box of tissues and a handheld mirror. Ginger started to open the drawers on either side of the knee hole of the dressing table but stopped herself just in time. Fingerprints, she thought. Then she decided that was a ludicrous idea. Her guest had died because of some health issue. The thought that it could be anything else was ridiculous. Still, she left the drawers alone and got down on her knees. The most logical place to find a cell phone would be in a woman's purse and since Liberty's purse had fallen to the floor and spilled...

Ah, there it was, all the way in the back recess under the dressing table. Someone on the police force would catch the devil for this oversight.

Ginger reached into the dark corner and could just touch the iPhone. Finally, she got a clothes hanger from the armoire and fished it out. She stood and stared at the face of it. She debated with herself the wisdom of checking out the call log. Maybe it was a family member trying to reach Liberty. Ginger's thumb hovered over the large button briefly then she gave in to the impulse. The phone's screen sprang to life at her touch. Not password protected, then.

She went to the log and looked at the incoming calls. A number labeled Boss showed seven calls. Ginger clicked on the messages and listened to an increasingly angry voice demanding that Liberty check in with the office. In the last message her boss said, "The federal government isn't paying you to be on vacation. And don't try to deny it. I've seen the photos plastered all over Facebook. Call me if you still want to have a job when you get back to D.C.!"

This was an interesting turn of events, Ginger thought. She flipped through the icons and opened Facebook. There, bigger than life, was Liberty Anderson, smiling for the camera. Ginger scrolled through several posts. She understood what had Liberty's boss so angry if she was, in fact, in Key West on business. Without question, a lot of partying had occurred.

She switched from Facebook to the camera on the phone. At the twelfth picture in, she stopped. There staring at her was a photograph of Trout. He was at a bar somewhere. She couldn't tell where, but he was smiling at the camera.

Ginger sat on the side of the bed and let the hand holding the phone rest in her lap as she stared into space. Trout hadn't told her that he knew Liberty. Which, in her opinion, would have been a given since the two of them found her dead on the morning he was supposed to take her out in his boat.

Her mind raced through what she knew of Liberty. Ginger had assumed she was in Key West on vacation. All her actions indicated that to be the case. And, yes, people in town for work usually took the time to see the sights and enjoy themselves, but Ginger hadn't thought that was the case with Liberty. She had slept in, dressed in shorts and halter tops or playful sundresses. So, what was this job?

Ginger went back to the phone for any clues. Most of the phone numbers had a D.C. area code. A few were local numbers, probably restaurants or tourist attractions. Liberty's Facebook page was a testament to the fact that she had hit just about every spot from Mallory Pier to the Southernmost Point marker. Few tourists had the stamina for that much partying except kids. Liberty was young but she wasn't a kid.

The photos on the camera were some of the same ones posted on Facebook but there were tons of others. A lot of them were of the Hemingway House Museum and the Hemingway cats. In fact, there were dozens of photos of cats all over Key West.

It was the shots of Westward Harbor Marina at the beginning of the string of pictures of Key West that stilled Ginger's scrolling finger. Trout docked at the Westward Harbor Marina and while there was no photo of his boat, it was odd that Liberty would photograph that particular marina, and so early in her stay. Had she gone looking for a boat to charter? Had Trout met her four days ago? She thought back over their conversation of the morning. It was true that he never specifically said he didn't know his fare, but it was implied. She had to find out why he had lied to her.

Ginger stood and ran a hand along the bed to smooth where she had been sitting. She slipped the phone into her back pocket, glanced around the room, and left. As she was locking the Toucan Suite, a door toward the back end of the landing opened and Annette Benoit stepped into the hallway.

"*Bonjour*," Annette said as she passed Ginger. At the top of the stairs, she turned back and asked. "Any calls for me?"

"No." Ginger picked up the stack of clean linens. "Still no calls."

The woman nodded and went down the stairs.

Ginger's heart thumped in her chest like a machine gun. She would never make a secret agent, she decided. The thought of getting caught in the act, of trespassing where she had been told specifically to leave under lock and key, had scared the pants off her. Would Annette think anything of her coming out of the Toucan Suite? Probably not. Annette was too caught up in her own situation, whatever that was, to pay attention.

She waited until she heard the front door of the Paradise close behind her guest. She returned the linens to the hallway table and hurried down the stairs. At the back of the bed and breakfast she had her personal quarters with a small office nook. She settled into her desk chair and scrolled down the numbers in Liberty's phone.

Her laptop was slow to boot up but finally the Google search page sprang onto the screen. She sat back in the chair. What was she doing? She should immediately call Duncan and tell him about the phone. It should be in the hands of the police. There was probably a simple explanation of why Liberty had a photo of Trout. The truth was, Ginger couldn't think of one. Because she couldn't think of a reason for a dead woman to have a photo of Trout and the marina where he docked his boat, she had to find out what Liberty had been doing in Key West. She didn't stop to question why it was so important to her to know.

On her laptop, Ginger keyed in a search for the first

of the local numbers in the phone's log. She needed to know where Liberty had been and what she'd been doing. Callahan hopped onto the desk and watched the computer screen.

"Where'd you come from?" Ginger asked as she scratched between his ears. "I haven't seen you in hours."

Callahan stretched his head in the direction of her magic fingers then settled into her lap, apparently bored with the scrolling letters on the computer screen.

Chapter Three

Trout blew a fine layer of sawdust from the mahogany plank and ran his hand along the smooth wood. To pay his dockage fees he helped Sawyer around the marina with manual labor. Sawyer's current passion was a vintage 1930s-era J class sailboat built by the Defoe Boat Works. Trout had been sanding the deck for two weeks.

He straightened from his task and as he wiped his cramped fingers with a rag, he let his gaze travel over the long line of docked boats. Walking down the pier toward him was Ginger, the afternoon sun creating a fiery halo of her dark red curls. Behind her trotted the strange looking cat from the Paradise.

Trout sighed, dusted the fine powder from the front of his shirt and shorts. This was not a good thing. He swung down the ladder to the pier and watched her approach. When she was still ten feet from him, she stopped.

"Why didn't you tell me?" she asked.

"Tell you what?"

"That you knew Liberty."

"Because it had nothing to do with the situation."

"So, you thought it would be better for me to be blindsided?" Her stance was defiant, a real squared off, no nonsense posture.

"Look," Trout said, "I don't know what the detective told you but—"

"Duncan didn't tell me anything."

Trout hesitated. "Then how…?" He angled his head a little to the right in a puzzled look.

"It doesn't matter how I know. You should have told me."

"Why?"

"Because…" she shook her head, raised and dropped her hands in a helpless gesture. "Because she's dead."

Trout glanced toward the shore and the marina office then returned his gaze to Ginger. "Come on," he motioned with his hand back down the pier from the direction she had come. "Let's find a little privacy, okay?"

Ginger stepped to the side so he could pass by her, and they walked about fifteen yards to where his boat, the *Baby Buddha*, was berthed. After a slight hesitation, Ginger climbed aboard. Trout nodded toward a canvas deck chair then went below. He came back on deck with two cold bottles of beer. He handed one to her and sat in the other chair.

"Now," he said, "tell me what you think you know."

Ginger shook her head. "It doesn't work that way, Trout. You need to tell me how you know Liberty Anderson. Tell me why a party girl chartered a fishing expedition. Why you?"

Trout nodded. "Good enough." He settled into his chair, his feet up on the transom, and faced the westerly sun. "Sawyer got a call from a woman wanting the use of a deep-water boat for a morning trip into the Gulf. She wasn't interested in fishing, just needed the transport and privacy. She wanted a sunrise kind of experience she told him. He gave her my number. He knew I could use the money." Trout took a long pull on his beer, wiped the back of his hand across his mouth, and continued. "She told me she would pay the regular fee for a half-day fishing excursion."

"If she wasn't interested in fishing, what was the purpose?"

Trout shook his head but continued to gaze into the distance. "Can't say. Maybe she just liked being out on the ocean. Maybe she wanted to commune with nature. I didn't ask."

"Why didn't you tell me you knew her?"

"Because I didn't. At least, I didn't know I knew her until I saw her sprawled across the bed." He took another drink then started peeling the label on the beer bottle. "The only contact I had with her was a phone call. At least, that's what I thought, until I looked into the room. I'd been sitting at the bar at the Bull and Whistle when she came in last night. She was in high spirits, friendly to a fault, taking pictures with her phone with everyone in the place. When she sat next to me, she asked me to smile, and she snapped my picture. Said her name was Alice."

When Trout said nothing more, Ginger prodded him. "And?"

"And nothing. Other people came in, she got involved

with them for a bit, bought drinks, took lots of pictures, and then she left."

Ginger's forehead creased into frown lines. "So, she just said, hi, my name is Alice. That's it?"

"Pretty much," Trout said.

"What happens in Vegas."

Trout cut his eyes in her direction. "My thoughts exactly."

"Still, that's a strange coincidence."

"The cops think so too."

"I don't know why you didn't tell me this morning."

Trout was silent. Finally, he heaved a heavy sigh, took another drink, and said, "I know how these things go. I didn't want to be in that position again. I thought that the autopsy would show she had some kind of condition, or maybe alcohol poisoning. She was drinking heavily and already tipsy when she got to the Bull and Whistle. I figured if I just kept my mouth shut, things would sort themselves."

"You said *again*. What does that mean?"

He pulled a long strip of the label from the bottle and let it drift to the deck of the boat. "Another girl, another death, another lifetime. It didn't matter that I didn't have anything to do with what happened to her, either. The police thought it was too much of a coincidence that I was her therapist and that I found her body."

"I'm sorry."

Trout emptied the bottle with one last chug, set it on the deck, and leaned further back in the chair, his eyes closed. "Yeah, well, that's life."

* * *

I don't doubt Ginger has many questions concerning Trout's reference to other girls and other deaths. My ability to judge character, however, is spot on. I'd prefer to know the facts, but on the face of things I can't think Trout is our killer. Still, it doesn't hurt to investigate every possibility. I could be wrong in my assessment of him. More likely, I'm wrong in thinking I could be wrong for I am pretty much infallible. It's not that I have a swelled head or anything like that. It's just a fact. Pity that so few people know about my crime solving abilities other than Dax. And he's certainly not one to broadcast the fact. He's fond of the saying "keep your powder dry." I'm more inclined to believe that it's better not to hide your light under a bushel. Ego had nothing to do with it. Mostly.

I think I'll take a stroll around the Baby Buddha *while Ginger and Trout await the sunset. They seem comfortable in the silence that has fallen over them since his revelation. I sense questions on Ginger's part but she's content for the moment to wait. Patience, a good skill for a detective to have. I confess I find her reaction to the situation and her instincts so far to be superior to that of the local authorities.*

The Baby Buddha *is a nice boat. Dax would love it. He's been keen on boats since we hit Florida. Camping on the beaches along our way to the Keys has been very pleasant and educational.*

Trout's boat isn't as large as a convertible, but still, it has a flying bridge and a cuddy cabin that's more roomy than some. Two people could sleep quite comfortably here for a night or two as long as the water wasn't too rough. Humans don't have the natural agility and inner balance that cats rely on to keep motion from being a problem.

There's nothing of interest below deck except a padlocked cabinet in the galley beneath the banquet seat. Probably where Trout stores valuables when his boat's unattended. I can't say I have much faith in the lock to the cabin proper. With all this valuable fishing gear on board I'd expect something more substantial. Then, again, I guess since Trout makes this his home, there isn't too much to worry about. He seems adequate to deal with anyone cruising the docks for an easy score. That and the fact that access to the pier requires a code should deter all but the most desperate.

From the flying bridge of the Baby Buddha *there's a nice view of the marina. I think I could become accustomed to life on the sea. Perhaps it's only the temptation of the contents of the live well that has me thinking such thoughts. I hope there's fish for dinner.*

* * *

Ginger and Trout finished their beers and she refrained from questioning him about his past or anything she had learned from Liberty's phone. She struggled with whether or not to tell him about finding it, and with her indecision about turning it in to Duncan. As the sun set below the horizon, she still hadn't made up her mind.

She was reluctant to disturb the harmony they had found. The truth was that she liked his nearness, liked the gentle bounce of the boat. When Trout refused her invitation to walk back to the Paradise for dinner, he declined without any excuses as to why. Good enough, she thought. It had been a rough day for both of them.

Callahan padded along beside her as she wound her way through the streets of Key West, taking the shortest route back to her bed and breakfast. She hadn't noticed him following her when she left the Paradise earlier in the day. Her mind had been so caught up with the happenings of the morning that it hadn't occurred to her to be more aware.

She wondered if Dax would be concerned about his absence but decided probably not. They were an interesting pair of traveling companions. She had known vagrants to have dogs for pets but never a cat. And Dax wasn't exactly a vagrant. He was, in fact, very skilled at odd jobs. He seemed to know a little about a lot of things. For that, she was thankful. The Paradise had a lot of needs and she had very little extra money. A skilled carpenter who knew a bit about plumbing and electrical issues who would work for a fraction of what the contractors in the Keys were willing to accept was a Godsend.

Now, as they made their way home, she decided Callahan was a smart cat, smart enough to follow her lead. He was probably hungry, too. She'd have to see what she could whip up for him.

Jules looked up from the book he was reading at the reception desk when she and Callahan came through the door. "Hi," he said. "There's a couple of messages for you from Detective Moore." He held out two pink slips of paper.

"Thanks. Everything else quiet?"

"Everything except the Bird Nest. She's called down twice asking if she's had any messages." He rolled his eyes. "As if I wouldn't put the call through."

"Doesn't she have a cell phone? I distinctly remember seeing her use one a couple of days ago."

"I think so." Jules scratched his beard. He had little facial hair and was trying desperately for a hippie look. "Maybe she doesn't want whoever it is to know her cell number. Some people don't like their number to get spread around."

"Maybe," Ginger said, her mind already distracted from the habits of her guest as she looked down at the pink message slips. "She is French, after all."

"So?"

"Ever been to Martinique?"

"Right." Jules grinned. "'*Do not bother me simply because you are a guest spending your money in my place of business and you have been waiting for your drink order for thirty minutes. You do not speak French and are therefore beneath my contempt. And when I finally condescend to bring you the wrong order, I will run after you and curse you in French for not leaving a tip.*'" Jules' accent and tone were dead on the money.

Ginger laughed. "Exactly. But be nice to her if you want a paycheck this week."

"You should have charged those jerks for the days remaining on their reservations. It's not like they're in danger from ghosts or anything."

"I can't afford to have bad reviews popping up on travel websites. Let's just hope none of them decide to share their 'harrowing, near death experience' online."

"How bad are things?" Jules looked truly alarmed.

Ginger smiled at his expression and shook her head. "Not that bad, for Pete's sake. But it would be nice to do more than break even. I'm trying to finish the reno on the garage apartment and I'd like to get it done this year. It would help with taxes, among other things."

"I don't need to be polishing off my resume, then?"

"Nope. I'm going to fix something to eat. You want anything?"

"I can always eat."

"Okay." Ginger stuffed the messages in her pocket. "I'll see what's in the fridge."

The cat was ahead of her, waiting impatiently in the doorway to the kitchen. "I think Callahan's hungry," she said as she crossed the foyer.

"Cats," Jules said. "There were two from the Hemingway

house out by the back patio earlier this evening. I thought they were supposed to be locked up at night."

Callahan pricked his ears forward then zoomed through the door to the dining room and the kitchen beyond. He was out of sight in a flash.

"They're harmless," Ginger said. "It's just some dumb government regulation. No one pays any attention to it anymore."

When Ginger entered the kitchen, Callahan was pacing by the back door. "Yeow," he complained. "Yeow."

"What? We were just outside. Aren't you hungry?"

Callahan scratched at the door.

"Fine." Ginger crossed the kitchen and opened the door. The cat took off and disappeared into the low lighting of the back garden of the Paradise. "Crazy cat," she said. She started to turn back into the kitchen then thought better of it. What if he wandered off? If there were other cats on the grounds, would he stray with them?

She went onto the back porch and called his name. Not a leaf rustled in the deep foliage. "Great." Ginger set off along the pathway that wound through the back garden. After a thorough search, she gave up. Callahan was nowhere to be found, not hiding under the lounge chairs by the pool, or anywhere near the tiki bar. She pondered what to do, then decided the best way to a cat's heart was the same as a man's. Food. When she entered the kitchen, she left the back door open just enough for him to squeeze through. Tonight's menu would definitely be fish.

* * *

Trout was finishing his second beer when he decided

he should have taken Ginger up on her invitation. She never told him how she knew about his encounter with Liberty. How could she have known, he wondered. Maybe the detective told her after all. Now he looked guilty in her eyes and that bothered him more than the suspicions of the police.

He debated opening a third beer but thought better of it. He hadn't eaten anything since the blueberry muffin and coffee at the Paradise. The wisest course would be to get something to eat. A perusal of his pantry and refrigerator produced nothing but beer, a rotting tomato, some iffy yogurt, and dried pasta. He was light in the pockets, but he decided he could manage a meal at the Smokin' Tuna. Maybe Ginger hadn't started cooking dinner yet. Maybe she would want to join him. Maybe not. He took another beer from the mini fridge and popped the top. He wasn't really that hungry.

Chapter Four

All of Megs' and Bartholomew's ramblings about secret agents and court orders now makes some sense. At least it's not so stream-of-consciousness now that I have an idea of what's at the heart of the matter. The question is, do they think there's a real threat from discovery in their wanderings or is what Ginger said the truth of the situation; that no one is concerned about enforcing the restrictions on the Hemingway cats? I can't see how this could play into the murder of Liberty Anderson, but my namesake wouldn't ignore the possibility so neither will I.

First, I'll check the little fire escape landing on the east side of the house. I get the impression it's a favorite spot for Megs and Bartholomew. Now, as I see it at night, I realize it's quite a good vantage point for two-thirds of the grounds of the Paradise.

The pool glimmers with underwater lights. It's a small pool, more for cooling off from the summer heat, I should think, than actually swimming. Still, I guess it allows Ginger to advertise it as an amenity.

No one is sitting at the alfresco tables or on the stools at the tiki bar. With only two of the seven rooms of the bed and breakfast occupied, I can understand why. Mademoiselle Benoit has gone out for the evening. I'm not sure about the Talents.

If only I could figure out how to get onto the gallery that runs along the front of the building I could discover if they're in their room. I could also learn if that's how the killer gained access to Liberty's room. I see no easy way to scale the side of the building. There isn't even a trellis for roses or whatever blooming thing that grows out of control here in the tropics.

The fire escape window is secure from access from the outside, that I know. One of the policemen checked the internal locking mechanism this morning. There's no evidence it's been tampered with from the outside. Even if it had, the killer would still need to gain entry into Liberty's room. A room that was most assuredly locked from the inside this morning.

There's no sign of life on the grounds of the property except for Ginger who is intent on finding me. As soon as she returns to the kitchen, I'll hustle down the stairs and go to the Hemingway House. If Megs and Bartholomew aren't here, then surely, they're there.

* * *

Ginger sealed the container of freshly cut fruit for the next morning's breakfast and stored it in the enormous refrigerator. She loaded the coffeemaker and set out clean cups and saucers, spoons, a variety of sweeteners, and a stack of bread-and-butter plates for pastries.

She picked up Callahan's plate of sautéed trigger fish with butter and capers sauce and covered it with wrap. She hoped he showed up before she closed up for the night. With everything else that was going on right now, the last thing she needed was a lost cat. Perhaps she was worrying too much about him. After all, he and Dax lived life on the road. It was obvious Dax wasn't concerned with Callahan's wanderings. They were camping out in the unfinished garage apartment until the job was finished. That's where the cat probably was.

She expelled a sigh. Finding him on an island crawling with cats would take a major stroke of luck and be darn near impossible. She kept reminding herself that he was smarter than the average cat according to Dax. All she could do was hope that meant he could find his way back to the Paradise if he had indeed wandered off.

Halfway through dinner with Jules, she also remembered that the Flamingo Suite still hadn't been made up. It was tempting to leave it until morning, but she knew that was a sure path to chaos. A convention was arriving in town on Wednesday, and she would be totally booked. It was best to stay on top of things when she had the time. The energy to do so was another story, but it had to be done. She would put a call in to Gabriella tomorrow to be sure she could help fill in for the duration of the full house.

As she finally closed the door on the clean and tidy Flamingo Suite, Ginger rubbed the ache in the back of her neck. She looked at the hallway clock. Eleven forty-five. When she reached the foot of the stairs, she glanced at the partially closed door to the office cubby behind the registration counter. Jules was propped up on the daybed, his book lying open across his chest, and his head back against the pillows in sleep.

She had heard the Talents come in while she was

making the bed in the Flamingo Suite. The key board at the front desk showed Annette Benoit's key still on the hook. Ginger frowned and shook her head.

She switched the front door of the Paradise to auto lock and dimmed the porch lights. A swipe pad would allow her errant guest to gain entry when she returned. In the event a guest was too intoxicated or couldn't find their key card, there was a buzzer that would rouse Jules.

It had been a long day, and she was ready to hit the sack. As she crossed the foyer to the hallway leading to her private rooms, she heard a muffled thump from upstairs. Callahan, she thought. He must have come in while she was in the Flamingo Suite. The crazy cat was obsessed with the Toucan Suite, had been even before they found Liberty's dead body.

She went up the curving staircase and turned in the direction of the noise she had heard. Out of the dim light from the wall sconces, a dark image sprang up from the doorway of the Toucan Suite and slammed into her, knocking her against the landing banister where she hit her head on the newel post. The intruder streaked past her and was headed down the stairs before Ginger's body hit the floor. She felt a sharp pain near her temple and knew she was losing consciousness.

* * *

Trout sat for an hour or more vacillating on the merits of breaking into his contingency fund. It was a hard call, one he had determined he wouldn't make except in dire circumstances. Then he thought about Liberty Anderson, dead while on holiday in paradise, and decided life was short.

He opened the locked cabinet under the banquet and took out a once expensive but now battered wallet. It contained ten one-hundred-dollar bills. He paused, fingering the bills then took one and slipped it into his pocket before leaving the dock in search of food.

He sat at the bar and ate the plate of fish tacos the Smokin' Tuna was known for and washed them down with his fourth beer of the evening.

At some point in the past year and a half he had started counting when he started drinking. It was his own method of self-regulation. There were days when he didn't drink anything. Sometimes those days would turn into a string that didn't end for a couple of weeks or more. Three beers were a bad day, he decided. A six pack was a really crappy day. He was contemplating a fifth beer when the detective, Duncan, waltzed in off the street to the outdoor bar at the Smokin' Tuna.

This was turning into a really crappy day, Trout decided. Duncan zeroed in on him and joined him.

"Been looking for you," Duncan said.

"Why's that?"

"You're an interesting guy, Armentrout Richardson." Duncan sat on the stool next to Trout and motioned for the bartender. When she leaned across to him, he ordered a vodka tonic.

Trout waited. He knew the policeman would get to the point in his own good time. There was always a point to be made in these situations, he thought.

"A charter boat captain is a big career change for a man like you, don't you think?"

"How so?"

Duncan shrugged in that funny way he had. "All that education, white collar job, soft hands. Seems to me like a big change."

"If you're going to make a change, it might as well be a big one."

"I suppose." Duncan took a sip of his drink. "I imagine you had more than enough reason." He looked at Trout. "The suicide and all. Wait. Not one suicide but two, isn't that right?"

"What is it you really want to say, detective?"

"I like Ginger. She's good people."

"I like her, too."

"I don't think you're hearing me." Duncan banged his glass down on the bar. "I think you spell trouble and Ginger doesn't need any more crap in her life."

"Two things." Trout stood, took the hundred-dollar bill from his pocket, and signaled for his check. "First, I hardly know Ginger and therefore am not an issue in her life one way or the other." The bartender made change for him. "And second." He left a tip and crammed the rest of the money into his pocket. "I like to eat alone." He headed toward the exit.

Duncan's phone rang on Trout's parting shot and he answered with a clipped, "Yes." After a split second he said, "What?" He was already moving past Trout to the street. "How bad is she?" He opened the door of a double-parked unmarked sedan. "Lock down the Paradise. Don't let so much as a mouse in or out until I get there."

Trout caught the door of the car as Duncan tried to close it. "It's Ginger, isn't it?"

Duncan jerked the door closed as he started the car. He tore away from the curb on squealing tires.

Trout started to run. It was three blocks to Petronia Street. He reached the Paradise just minutes after Duncan.

* * *

I can't believe I didn't see this coming. Clearly whoever killed Liberty didn't get what he was after. This is his handiwork. I know it in my bones. His scent still lingers though it's growing faint.

It pained me to return to the Paradise and this, the back door open, Jules asleep on the job, and Ginger badly wounded. I don't know how long she's been out but thank goodness she's coming around. At least Jules isn't a heavy sleeper. He came the instant I called out and has been on the phone with emergency services and the police.

Ginger groans and holds her head. Jules is back at her side.

"Don't move, Ginger. The paramedics are on the way."

"I'm okay…" *she tries to rise then slumps back onto the carpet runner of the upper landing and groans again.* "My head."

The police are banging at the door and Jules runs down the stairs to trip the lock and let them in. Paramedics are on their heels, medical cases in hand. I heave a sigh of relief.

The Talents come out of their room, swaddled in bath robes. A policeman shoos them back inside and asks them to wait until they determine the situation. I foresee another departure from the Paradise come morning.

The paramedics have barely begun to minister to Ginger's wound when Detective Moore appears on the scene. His face is white with concern or rage, I'm not sure which at this point. He kneels beside her and pushes her hair from her face.

"Hey, kiddo. What's going on?"

She smiles then winces. "I'm not sure. I heard a noise and came upstairs. I thought it was the cat." *She closes her eyes.*

"Ginger?" *Duncan's voice is sharp.*

The paramedic pushes him aside. He forces Ginger's eye open and checks it with a penlight.

"Stop." *Ginger whispers as she turns her head to the side, away from the probing light.* "I'm okay." *She licks her lips.* "It hurts to talk."

"Get her to the hospital," *Duncan says.*

Ginger grabs his arm. "No. I need to be here."

"You've got a head injury. Don't argue. You need a CT scan."

"The Paradise…"

"Jules can take care of things."

Tears begin to seep from beneath Ginger's closed eyelids. "Please, Duncan."

"Shit," *he says under his breath.* "Don't do that, Ginger. Just get the scan. If things are okay, you can come back home."

"I'll stay, Ginger." *Trout is standing over the men kneeling around Ginger. He's breathing heavy.*

She opens her eyes, then closes them and gives a faint nod.

The cops have the situation with Ginger in hand. I need to investigate before they turn their minds to the actual crime scene and start mucking about in things. The door of the Toucan Suite is closed. I can't say whether or not it's still locked. If only I had an opposable thumb! Where are Megs and Bartholomew when they might actually be of help? Oh, well, I'm sure this will be checked by the bipeds before much longer. I'll move on to other things. Important things. Like access.

I trot down the hallway and around the corner, past the Bird Cage and linen closet to the emergency exit window. Its lock is still secure. That means nothing, of course, as it automatically locks when closed. Still, I know our intruder didn't enter that way or it would be broken. There's an absence of the scent that hovered on the landing when I first arrived on the scene. I don't think our culprit left this way either. Obviously, the back door is the point of entry and escape.

Downstairs I find the door to Ginger's quarters is ajar. His scent is here. My blood boils with the realization that he violated her personal space. If she had been in her room the circumstances might be much worse than they are.

Our killer is definitely looking for something. He has been through her desk. It was a tidy job, but very thorough. The good news is that he didn't recognize Liberty Anderson's cell phone. It sits smack in the middle of the desktop where Ginger left it. I must gain access to whatever information it holds, but how? I will leave it for now. Best to check the exterior of the Paradise to see if our marauder left any useful clues.

Say now, what's this? It appears our villain waited for his opportunity behind the tiki hut. The shutters are askew. It's a good spot from which to monitor the activities of the bed and breakfast. It's even better that the two cabins back here are unoccupied.

From this vantage point the intruder could be sure of privacy and be able see down the side of the building to the steps leading onto the front porch. Anyone coming or going would be noticed. The whole backside of the Paradise is visible, the kitchen on full display through the undraped window. He had an unobstructed view of the dining room through the bay window and of Ginger's quarters, lit from within by a desk lamp. All the villain had to do was wait and watch.

A rustling sound comes from the bed of cast iron plants, and I crouch, ready to spring. It's only Megs and Bartholomew.

"Where have you been?" *I ask.*

"Here and there," *Bartholomew answers.*

"Doing what?"

"This and that." *He's momentarily distracted by a moth.*

"No one saw us," *Megs says.*

"Saw you doing what?"

She doesn't answer my question, instead she sidles up beside me, purrs, and bats her eyelashes. "Whatcha doin' out here, Callahan?"

"Looking for a killer."

"The one with the strange smell?" *She nuzzles my ear.*

I twitch my ears and shake my head as I back away. "You've seen him?"

Bartholomew clears his throat, "Seen who? Neither saw nor been seen. Not me, not Megs."

"Enough!" *I say.* "This is serious business. A woman was killed last night."

"The spy." *Megs nods her head.* "It was bound to happen."

I've had enough of this cat and mouse game with Bartholomew and Megs. Either they've eaten too much mercury-laced tuna or they think they're penning a literary tale of the Alice in Wonderland *variety. I'll have some straight answers out of these two before the sun rises. It's time to charm the truth out of Megs if I can get past the thought of her strange, crossed eyes.*

* * *

The police didn't clear out of the bed and breakfast until well after two in the morning. The gray cat kept pace with Trout as he locked the front door behind the last of them and checked that the kitchen door was also secure. He took a stance in front of an empty bowl on the floor near the pantry and began to complain. Trout got the message and opened the large refrigerator. He spied the covered container of fish with some kind of sauce.

"Now I really am sorry I missed dinner," he said to the cat as he unwrapped the contents of the dish and slid it into Callahan's bowl. "I bet you'd like some water as well." Callahan didn't pause from his repast to comment. Trout grinned and took the bowl marked water and filled it.

Once the cat finished eating, he looked up at Trout as

he ran his tongue over his mouth and cleaned his whiskers. "What?" Trout asked. "In or out? Is that it?"

"Yeow," the cat said and took off across the kitchen to the hallway and then to the back of the bed and breakfast. He stopped and looked back at Trout when he came to a closed door at the end of the hall.

Trout watched him and the cat did the darnedest thing. He stretched up to the doorknob with his forepaws and scratched at it.

"What's this about?" He asked as he opened the door. Immediately he knew he was in Ginger's private quarters. When he stepped back into the hall, the cat streaked in and hopped onto the desk.

"Yeow," he said and with a flick of his paw sent a cell phone in the center of the desk spinning to the floor.

Trout retrieved the phone and when he replaced it on the desk, the cat yowled again.

"What's with you, crazy cat?" Trout tried to pick Callahan up to take him from the room and the cat hissed and bowed his back.

Once again, Callahan's paw whipped out and sent the phone flying across the room.

Trout looked from the cat to the phone. This time when he picked it up, he pushed the button and activated it. He wasn't sure what he was supposed to do but he felt certain the cat wanted him to do something. He felt a little ridiculous doing the cat's bidding, but he clicked on the call log anyway. It showed a bunch of numbers from a 202 area code. Trout knew that code, Washington, D.C. He looked at the messages, reading the script of the last one. It was then he realized this wasn't Ginger's phone. It belonged to Liberty.

The last message she received prompted him to open Liberty's Facebook page. As Ginger had before him, he went to her camera feature as well. So, this was how Ginger had known he was familiar with Liberty.

Trout sat at the desk and stared at the iPhone. It would be a simple thing to delete the photo. No one would be the wiser. Except Ginger. The question was, why did Ginger have Liberty's phone? Surely the police would have taken it with them when they came to investigate her death. Something was nagging at him about the why and how of this situation.

He glanced at the clock on the bedside radio. Nearly three in the morning. He was tired, his brain wasn't functioning as it should. What he needed was sleep but he had promised Ginger he would man the fort until she returned from the hospital. Jules was upset, blaming himself for the break-in. Maybe he could make him feel better, Trout thought. After a moment's hesitation, he wiped the phone on his shorts, returned it to Ginger's desk, and closed the door on her room, a struggling gray cat in his arms.

* * *

Ginger turned toward the sound of the door opening. Duncan put his head around it and said, "Hey, you decent?"

"Yes. Come in. What did you find?"

He rolled his shoulders in a shrug. "Nothing so far. I can't tell if he was trying to pick the lock on the murder room, or not, until you have a look-see. It could be all those scratches are from former guests having issues with sobriety."

"Could be," she said. "You said murder room?"

"It looks that way. At the very least, manslaughter. Her alcohol level was point two one eight, but the urine test also showed the presence of the date rape drug, GHB. A deadly combination. She was purposely drugged somewhere along her route of partying last night. Clearly there was intent to at least immobilize her."

"How could she make it back to her room if she was drugged?"

"It takes twenty minutes to an hour for a roofie to fully kick in. The problem is the time of death. She wasn't at the Paradise at one o'clock, that we know. Obviously, she came in at some point after that. The room was air conditioned, so the ME has to take that into consideration. Also, how long it took her to die. No way to determine that with any certainty."

"So, it was date rape?"

"Looks that way on the face of it but there's no evidence of actual sexual activity. Whoever it was must have gotten scared off or lost his nerve. Maybe he was afraid of getting caught coming or going from an establishment as small as the Paradise. Who knows."

Ginger knew she shouldn't feel such a sense of relief, but she did. Liberty's death was because she crossed paths with the wrong person. It didn't make the taint go away completely but as far as publicity goes, the same thing could have happened if she'd been staying at any other accommodation in Key West.

Her death had already made the local morning news coverage. No doubt there would be a write up in the *Key West Citizen*. If Ginger was lucky, the *Miami Herald* wouldn't pick up the story. She adjusted her position in the hospital bed and winced.

"What did the doc say about the crack on the head?"

"I'll live."

"I need a little more than that, Ginger."

"Some swelling, no intracranial bleeding, a few stitches. Nothing that won't right itself in a couple of days. The good news is that the paramedics packed my head with ice to keep the swelling at a minimum. Remind me to bake them a key lime pie."

"No bleeding, huh?"

"Nothing to worry about. Dr. Harrison says the body will take care of itself. I have a very hard head."

"True."

She laughed then grimaced. "Stop. I want to get out of here this afternoon."

"What time?"

"He said around one if I behave."

"I'll swing by and get you."

"You don't need to do that."

"Apparently, I do. Someone has to keep you out of trouble. Besides, you can take a look at the lock on the Toucan Suite and give me your opinion. See if anything else looks out of place, tell me if the tape was still intact the last time you noticed."

Ginger blushed crimson. "Oh. About that."

Duncan's brows shot up in a knowing look. "About that, what?"

"The tape. I cut it."

He said nothing for a long tick of the clock. "Why?"

"The phone. I could hear the phone ringing and, well, I went in to answer it."

When she said nothing else, he asked, "Don't keep me

in suspense. Who was it?"

"I don't know. I mean, I do, and I don't. The phone quit ringing as soon as I opened the door."

"So, explain to me how you do, and you don't, know who was calling."

"The call log. On her cell phone."

"You have her cell phone?"

"That's what I said."

"I thought you meant the room phone." "Oh." Ginger could see his temper rising. She hoped his wrath would be directed toward the underling who failed to find the iPhone when they searched Liberty's room. "It was under the dressing table. It must have fallen out of her purse."

"So, that's what he was after."

It took a second for Ginger to realize the implication of Duncan's comment and she understood why he was being so protective. Why the killer had returned to the Paradise hadn't been resolved to Duncan's satisfaction. Now there was a reason; to find Liberty's cell phone. His photograph must be among the party photos. What other explanation could there be? Then she remembered that Trout's picture was also on Liberty's phone.

Chapter Five

It's sometimes a chore to work with people. They haven't the instinctive skills of detection that come naturally to me: the hunter's instinct. It's often like their expression 'pulling teeth' to steer them where they need to go. And it's almost as painful. Ah, well, I must work with what I have. Right now, I need to get into the locked Toucan Suite. Ginger is safely home, and she and Duncan have brought Trout into their line of thought as to why Liberty died. I must make them understand that it's a false premise. Something more is going on here and right now I don't have a clue as to what.

Detective Moore has Liberty's cell phone. His hostility toward Trout is not helped by what he sees there.

"This was what time?"

Trout shrugs. "Eleven or so. I'm sure you have someone who can determine when the picture was taken. And you can ask Evan. He was tending bar. He'll probably remember. Approximately."

"This little party you mentioned, the one that was headed out to The Oriole, how do I know you didn't go with them?"

"You'll just have to take my word for it, I guess. And it wasn't a party headed that way, more like she was trying to talk it up."

Duncan grunts. He doesn't give the impression of someone willing to take Trout's word for anything.

"You knew this picture was on her phone?"

"Honestly, I didn't think about it. We crossed paths like people do in a bar. She stood out because she wanted to be noticed. At least that's the impression I got."

"That's your professional opinion, I take it," *Duncan says,* "as a psychologist."

Trout glances at Ginger then looks Duncan square in the eyes. "I observe people, form opinions, same as anyone else."

"Except you have a bunch of letters after your name that say you analyze people, see the patterns in their actions, predict their behavior."

Trout clinches his jaw then releases it. "No one can predict how any given individual will react to life's challenges. You simply work with them to get to the core of their pain, teach them options, coping mechanisms."

"Uh huh."

Ginger stirs on the sofa in the informal sitting room where she's lying. "Won't the pictures help you retrace her steps from that night?"

Ah, Ginger once again comes to Trout's rescue, distracting the detective from him. It's as I suspected; the heart trumps the head.

Duncan glances at Ginger. I can see he's drawing the same conclusion.

"Sure," *he says as he slips the phone into his coat pocket.* "We already have her credit card charges. This will help us recreate a timeline and start taking statements from anyone who might have seen her. We might even get lucky and find out if anyone was paying her particular attention. So far, we've had no luck reaching anyone at her home in Virginia. The local cops are going to check out the address for us. Maybe her boss can shed a little light on things. Now that I know about her boss."

Ginger blushes.

"You got a quiet spot where I can make some calls?" *he asks.*

"The desk in my quarters. There's a laptop as well if you need it." *Ginger sits up and swings her feet to the floor.*

"I can do what I need to with my phone. And you're supposed to be on bed rest."

'There's too much to do. There's a convention on Wednesday…"

"Forty-eight hours. Doctor's orders." *Duncan motions his head in Trout's direction.* "The shrink will see to the Paradise."

Trout crosses the room to Ginger. "Stop worrying. Jules and I have everything under control. We got breakfast with what was already in the refrigerator and the bread basket. The Talents have been given vouchers to the Smokin' Tuna for dinner as a goodwill gesture. Gabriella is cleaning their room as we speak." *He helps her to stand and turns her toward the back of the building.* "Everything's going to be fine but only if you allow yourself to mend."

Well, that worry is off my plate. As long as Duncan and Trout are sparring over Ginger, I know she'll get the care she needs. Trout seems to be getting through to her. A nice lie-down will do wonders for her. She's still quite pale.

Duncan heads for the empty dining room, his cell phone in one hand and Liberty's cell phone in the other. I'll just check that Ginger's room is secure then I'll see if I can prompt Trout to open the Toucan Suite.

The police are operating under the impression that the killer wasn't in Liberty's room, that she came back to the bed and breakfast alone and locked herself in her room. But I know better. The killer was in there. The question is whether or not he was in there when Liberty died.

I need to make them realize that even though the room was locked, he managed to gain access somehow. And I need to find whatever he was searching for. That's the key to this case. Once we know the what, we'll be able to determine the why, and track down the who.

* * *

Trout sent Jules home as soon as he settled Ginger in her bed and Duncan cleared out, talking on his cell phone the whole while.

Annette Benoit came breezing into the foyer. It was after two in the afternoon and Trout realized she had been out all night and most of the day. She had that elegantly disheveled look that many strive for, but French women so easily effect. Not my business, he thought. She collected the key to the Bird Cage room and swept up the stairs past the cat.

Callahan had been restless and vocal since Duncan's departure from the Paradise. Food wasn't the answer, and he didn't want to go out. He kept returning to the third step of the stairs leading up to the second floor, waiting, but not very patiently. Trout tried to ignore him, but the cat wasn't having it.

Trout listened to the sounds of Angela and Gabriella as they prepared the dining room for breakfast the next day. The murmur of their conversation and the clink of china and silverware created no demands on his concentration as his mind worried at the tangle of events swirling around the Paradise. His gaze settled on the cat.

"Yeow."

Trout noted that he tended to favor the third step of the stairs. Cats, a sudden death, numerology. He laughed at the direction his thoughts were taking. He got up from the stool behind the reception desk and turned down the hallway to Ginger's quarters to check on her.

It wasn't really a surprise to find her sitting at her dressing table examining the gash on her head. "You were meant to be resting."

"Can't sleep. Never have been one to nap during the day. Besides, all the medications they gave me in the wee hours this morning have worn off and I'm wide awake."

"How are you feeling?"

"Fine. A bit of a headache still but that's all."

"No blurry vision, dizziness?"

"Honestly. Between you and Duncan you'd think I was an invalid." Ginger stood and turned from addressing his image in the mirror of her dressing table to the real thing. "Mainly, I feel ticked off that someone thinks they can run amok at the Paradise, bashing people in the head, trespassing…" She paused. "That poor woman."

"Yeah." Trout jangled the change in his pocket. "How about a cup of coffee?"

"Maybe some tea?"

"Sure." He gave Ginger one last assessing look and

turned from the room.

Duncan and Ginger seemed convinced that the murderer had returned to the Paradise because he feared his image was on Liberty's phone. It sounded logical, it certainly fit the facts. Yet something about the whole thing bothered Trout. Something he couldn't put his finger on. He shook his head.

When Ginger entered the kitchen, Trout noticed she had brushed her hair. The way it formed a wave over the right side of her forehead hid the stitches. She looked good for someone who had been knocked unconscious a mere sixteen hours earlier.

He placed the steaming cup of tea and a plate of cookies in front of where she sat at the long kitchen worktable. For himself, he poured a cup of the coffee Angela had made to go with the afternoon cookies.

The cat came in from the lobby and began to complain to Ginger.

She reached down and scratched him under the chin. "What do you want? Are you hungry?"

"He's not hungry. He doesn't want to go out. He has plenty of water. He's just being a pain in the butt."

"Did you feed him?"

"Scrambled eggs with goat cheese and heavy cream."

"Wow." Ginger took a sip of her tea. "No one ever spoiled me like that."

"I couldn't find any cat food."

"I've been told Callahan doesn't eat cat food. He has a very discerning palate. He should be your best buddy after that feast."

"Well, there's no pleasing him. I thought cats slept twenty-three hours a day."

"That's dogs. He just wants to get into the Toucan Suite."

"How do you know?"

"I speak cat."

"Ha, ha." Trout took one of the sugar cookies from Ginger's plate. "So, tell me about Duncan."

"What about him?"

Trout noticed that the question brought a spot of color to Ginger's cheeks. "You two seem to know each other pretty well."

"We're both conchs, born on the island, always lived on the island except for about six years for me. We've known each other all our lives, went to school together. He's a friend."

"It seems like more."

Ginger turned the tea cup around and around on the table top. She sighed. "It was, for a while. A very short while. And it was a mistake. Now we're just trying to be what we once were, friends."

She stopped turning the cup and looked up at Trout. "A psychologist, huh?"

"For a while. A long while, actually. It was a mistake. Now I'm a charter boat captain."

"Seems like there's more to it than that."

When Trout didn't say anything, Ginger waited.

Finally, he said, "I worked for the state, Department of Children and Families. In Tallahassee. My patients were the runaways, the throwaways, and the forgotten." He stood and emptied his cup of cold coffee in the sink. "There aren't a lot of success stories in that line of work. After a while you're either just going through the motions or it grinds you down."

The cat was once again under his feet, twining between his legs. "Yeow."

"What?"

Ginger stood and brought her tea cup to the sink. "I think we should see what's in the Toucan Suite."

* * *

The Toucan Suite held the scent of abandonment, Ginger thought as she opened the door. It had only been vacant one day, yet it seemed so void of life, as if it had been empty for a long time. Perhaps that's what sudden death does to a space, she thought.

Trout used the toe of his tennis shoe to swing the door to the bathroom open. "When did they say you could clean the room?"

"They, meaning Duncan, didn't say. I'll have to give him a call and ask. I have a reservation for this room in three days."

"She was leaving in three days?"

"She was leaving tomorrow." Ginger decided to follow Trout's example. She took a tissue from the dispenser on the dressing table and used it to safeguard against leaving any prints and opened the armoire.

Something about the decision to take such precautions made her heartbeat accelerate. There was no reason for it to do so, she told herself. The mystery of Liberty's death had been resolved. She died from a combination of alcohol and drugs. End of story. This was a room in the Paradise, her bed and breakfast. Decades of polishing this furniture, cleaning this bathroom, checking the armoire and the highboy for forgotten items through the years of ownership by her grandmother, her mother, and now herself, made it as familiar to her as her own rooms.

"You okay?"

Trout's question, spoken so near, made her jump. He had moved from a perusal of the bathroom to her side without her realizing it.

"Sorry. Didn't mean to spook you."

She tried for a smile. "I'm being silly. I guess it's the idea that someone died at the Paradise, right here in this room."

"A natural reaction. Anyone else ever die here?"

"My grandmother. Other than that, I don't know. Logic would suggest that there have been deaths here over the long history of the house but none that I'm aware of."

He nodded and turned his attention to Callahan, who crawled out from under the bed and sat on his haunches and stared into space. "Looks like he didn't find what he wanted," Trout said.

"He does seem disappointed."

Trout moved to the floor-to-ceiling windows on the far side of the room. The furniture arrangement created a path to one of them so guests would have easy access to the gallery. He checked that it was locked, then unlocked it and raised it. It gave a familiar low squeal as the pulley weights hidden in the window casing lowered to raise the sash.

Trout stepped out onto the gallery. The cat followed him, sniffing the threshold and the immediate area of the wide, covered space. Once again Callahan sat and stared out into the distance. Ginger watched both cat and man for several seconds. Both seemed lost in thought. She stepped through the window and joined them.

Trout stood near the railing, his hands in his pockets, and seemed miles away. Callahan glanced at Ginger then walked along the gallery, investigating each window that opened onto it. Three rooms of the Paradise had access to this inviting space in the same manner as the Toucan Suite. The middle room, the Flamingo Suite, was vacant, the occupants having been the first to depart in the wake of Liberty's death. The Talents occupied the Macaw Suite, the last of the rooms that could be accessed from this gallery.

Ginger settled into one of the outdoor chaise lounges and closed her eyes. The deep shade of the roof overhang made this a perfect idyll for guests willing to pay the higher rate for one of these rooms. She listened to the sound of tourists passing along the street below as they debated what to see next. The faint skittering of claws alerted her that Eddie the Iguana had appeared on the scene, checking to see who had invaded his aerie. A sense of calm spread over her and for the first time in two days she began to relax.

When Ginger opened her eyes, she realized the day was fading. She turned to see Trout in the chaise lounge beside her, Callahan curled at his feet. She pushed herself into a more upright position.

"Sorry. I must have dozed off."

"You needed the rest."

"Have you been here the whole while?"

"Pretty much. I went down to talk to Angela. She's manning the front desk."

"Thanks."

"I've been thinking."

"About?"

"You remember telling me you caught a scent of something in Liberty's room?"

Ginger stretched her arms over her head and stifled a yawn. "It had a sweetness to it."

"Huh." Trout grew quiet for several seconds. "Have you ever smelled it before?"

"I'm not sure. At the time it seemed familiar, but I couldn't place it. I wasn't even sure I'd smelled anything after that first instant when I opened the door. It was such a fleeting sensation."

"But it was something you thought to be out of the ordinary for a woman's room?"

"I guess." Ginger swung her legs over the side of the chaise lounge and stood. "Why?"

Trout unfolded his long frame from the other lounger and stood also, disturbing Callahan in the process. "I don't know. Something feels off. I can't put my finger on it."

Ginger felt a thread of apprehension creep along her spine at his words. She rubbed her arms against a non-existent chill in the late August afternoon. "Let's hope not. I don't need any more trouble."

"Right."

They stepped back through the tall window opening into the Toucan Suite. Trout closed and locked it. Ginger didn't linger in the room. As soon as Trout and Callahan came through the door, she started to pull it closed. Her eyes skimmed over the room one last time and stopped at the highboy. Sitting atop it was something that didn't belong there.

* * *

At last Trout has seen the light. Or at least begun to listen to his instincts. Neither he nor Ginger have been quick off the mark on this case but then they are merely humans. I do believe, however, something has caught her eye.

"Trout," *she pushes the door wide and steps back into the room. He turns at the odd sound of her voice and joins her.* "What?"

"There. On top of the highboy. That doesn't belong in this room."

"Where does it belong?"

"I don't know. I've never seen it before."

All three of us stare at the silk covered rectangular box atop the highboy. The design is Asian. An ivory toggle serves to fasten it. After a second's pause, Trout reaches up and brings down the box that looks to be about six by eight inches.

"It's heavy."

Ginger eyes the elaborately decorated container but doesn't touch it. "It must belong to Liberty."

Trout places it on the dressing table. "This could be what the killer was after."

Ginger looks from the box to Trout and back. "We should call Duncan."

Neither of them makes a move to put her words into action. Now we're getting somewhere. If they'll only open the box. I jump onto the vanity and sniff at it. "Yeow." *There is no trace of the murderer's scent on the box which tells me he overlooked it. That makes me think he didn't recognize it as the object he sought. If it actually is what he was after. Surely it must be.*

"Yeow."

"Get down, Callahan." *Ginger lifts me from the vanity and deposits me on the floor.* "This is evidence."

I couldn't agree more but unless we open it, we won't know the motive for the crime. Detective Moore's concern for Ginger has raised my opinion of him but not so much his sleuthing skills. I must press the point if we are to make any progress. I jump back onto the vanity.

Trout grabs me and puts me out the door then closes it. I can't believe it! Doesn't he understand what's at stake? This is worse than Megs' description of the perp as a thin man with a lovely voice wearing a Hawaiian print shirt. Every other tourist in Key West is wearing a Hawaiian print shirt though the descriptive 'thin' does narrow the field considerably among today's American males. She did say the man's scent reminded her of Papa Hemingway. Another of her delusions and a dead end if there ever was one. Even with nine lives she couldn't have known Hemingway, considering the fact that he killed himself in 1961. Are we to believe the murderer is a ghost? Nonsense.

* * *

"We should open it," Trout said. "This might be the reason someone wanted to drug her."

"The police think Liberty was the target of date rape."

"So, no harm, no foul."

"If this is the reason Liberty died, we'd be tampering with evidence."

"We're not tampering with anything. The police left this along with the clothes in the armoire, Liberty's suitcase, and several pair of shoes. They didn't see any reason to process them as evidence."

"This is different. They looked through all her belongings and only took what they thought might have some bearing on what happened to her, her purse and its contents, her makeup. They were looking for an overdose or something that could be a source of poison. They even took her laptop." She worried her lower lip as she stared at the box that seemed to scream trouble. "No one would think this belonged to a guest. It looks like a purposeful decoration, something meant to be part of the room's furnishings."

"Exactly," Trout said. "The killer didn't take it for that reason. It looks like a fixture of the room. If the highboy wasn't so tall, you would have noticed it before now."

Ginger shook her head. "I think we should call Duncan."

"Fine." Trout took his cell phone from his back pocket and took a couple of photos of the box. "Call him. These shots will show it as we found it but I'm not waiting for him to open it."

"Trout…"

"Don't worry, Ginger. I won't touch anything. I just want to see what's inside." He took a tissue from the holder and slipped the ivory toggle from the embroidered slot. He glanced at Ginger then lifted the lid.

Inside the box was a clear plastic bag filled with what looked like gray sand.

Ginger released a sigh of relief and reached out to touch it. Trout caught her hand.

"I wouldn't if I were you."

"But it's nothing. Just some kind of dirt or…"

"If it's what I think it is, we'd best leave it for the police."

"What do you think it is?"

"Someone's cremated remains."

"Oh, my God." Ginger turned into Trout's chest and his arms came around her. "Oh, my God."

He held her for a long minute in a light embrace, allowing her the time to absorb the nature of their discovery. Finally, she pulled free of his arms and turned her face from him.

"Sorry. I'm just feeling a little overwhelmed, I guess."

"No problem. It wasn't what I was expecting either." He watched her compose herself and thought how easy it would be to get accustomed to holding her. She turned back to face him.

"We'd better call Duncan," she said.

"I should have listened to you." He jangled the change in his pocket. "I'm sorry."

"Waiting to learn what was in it from Duncan wouldn't have changed anything." She glanced around the room. "I don't know if I'll ever be able to get past two bodies in this suite. It'll never be the same."

"Try to look at the bright side. You can now qualify for the Ghosts and Gravestones tour."

"Not helping, Trout."

"Just trying to lighten the mood."

"The only thing that's going to lighten the mood is to find out what's going on at the Paradise."

"Agreed."

"So, how do we do that?"

"Maybe Duncan's made contact with Liberty's boss or a family member. I think we need to find out why she was in Key West. Maybe we can then figure out if her death is related to what she was doing here or if it has some other root cause."

Ginger took a tissue from the holder and gently lowered the lid of the box back in place. She didn't fasten the clasp. "My phone's in my room. I'll call Duncan. For now, I guess we should leave things as they are and lock the door."

"I think I'll stand guard on the landing." Trout regretted his words as soon as they were out of his mouth. The cloud of worry seemed to deepen in Ginger's expression.

"He'll want to know we had eyes on the situation until he gets here."

She merely nodded and headed down the stairs.

Callahan sat on a hall table, his golden gaze fixed on Trout.

"You should be happy now," Trout said to him.

Callahan leapt lightly to the floor and trotted down the stairs after Ginger.

"Fine," Trout said.

* * *

Duncan wasn't pleased when Ginger told him that she and Trout had opened the box. He arrived at the Paradise in less than fifteen minutes, a lab tech following on his heels.

"What the hell, Ginger?"

"Sorry, Duncan. We wanted to be sure it had any significance."

"Right." Her explanation did nothing to erase the glower on his face. "Do me a favor and let me be the judge of what has significance in the future."

"Sure." She watched him bound up the stairs followed by the CSI tech. After a moment of indecision, she climbed after him. She wasn't going to be left in the dark.

When she and Trout tried to enter the room after him, Duncan turned to them and barked, "Out."

Two uniformed policemen arrived along with another detective and an additional CSI tech. One of the policemen shooed Callahan away from the door of the Toucan Suite, then asked Ginger and Trout to wait downstairs in the sitting room. The look on Duncan's face when she protested their exclusion made her think twice. Reluctantly she and Trout descended to the lobby and waited.

The Talents returned from an excursion at the height of all the hubbub. Ginger held her breath for fear that they would demand to be checked out but instead they displayed mild curiosity and because they weren't allowed to go up to their room, decided to spend the wait time by the pool in the shade of the palm trees.

Harry, Ginger's part-time bartender, didn't come on duty until five when Ginger knew they were housing so few guests. Normally she could keep an eye on people lounging by the pool while she worked in the kitchen. She sent Angela to man the tiki bar with instructions to give the Talents whatever they wanted in an effort to defuse any further blowback. She then programmed the bed and breakfast's landline to transfer to her cell.

In short order, Annette Benoit came down the stairs in a huff, her late afternoon nap having been interrupted by the police demanding access to her room. Ginger didn't think free booze would soothe those ruffled feathers as Annette sailed through the Paradise to the courtyard.

When Duncan finally came downstairs, Ginger and Trout waylaid him. "Well?" she asked.

"Definitely burned remains. Probably human from the amount of ash. Most likely from a cremation, which would be the good news," Duncan said.

"And the bad news?" Ginger felt her heart thumping in her chest.

"It could be the barbeque variety."

Trout swore under his breath. "Jesus, could you be any more callous?"

Duncan looked at Ginger and what could have been

a shadow of regret swept briefly over his features. "Sorry. It's probably the former. We should be able to determine which in the lab."

"How?" Ginger asked.

"The evenness of the burn, if there's any other debris in the ash. That kind of thing."

"Great," Trout said.

"Yeah, well, the techie is pretty sure it's the former which makes my job easier. All we have to do is find out who in Ms. Anderson's life has died recently."

"Have you been able to contact her family?" Ginger asked.

"Not yet. Talked to the boss. He was hot under the collar about how she spent her time while here. Apparently, the USDA monitors their employees' social media. She worked for their enforcement branch. The purpose of her visit was supposed to be to determine if the Hemingway cats were in violation of the federal court order. Or rather that the management at the museum wasn't doing its job. Apparently, there'd been a complaint that the staff was being lax in following the AWA guidelines."

"Wait," Trout said. "What are you talking about? What does the Department of Agriculture have to do with cats?"

"The museum was sued some years back under the Animal Welfare Act because someone didn't think the cats were being properly cared for. That's under the jurisdiction of the USDA." Duncan shrugged. "They fought in the courts for years, but a decision was finally handed down in 2013, I think. The museum lost. So now they're monitored by the federal government."

"I can't believe what you're saying." Trout glanced at Ginger for confirmation. She nodded. "Were the museum cats being mistreated?"

"Of course not. They're the most pampered animals in the contiguous forty-eight states but you know how the government is. The urge to have a finger in every pie is like catnip to any regulating agency. And once they had a citizen's complaint it was all over but the shouting." Duncan took his pinging cell phone from his jacket pocket and read a message. "If you want to know my opinion, I think the Hemingway cats serve as an excuse for federal employees like Ms. Anderson to have a nice vacation in Key West on the government's dime."

"That would explain all the photos of the cats she took. I couldn't get my head around that because she didn't like cats," Ginger said.

"Perfect for the job, then." Duncan slipped his phone back into his pocket. "Look, I've got to head over to the station. Don't worry, Ginger, I'll let you know what we find out about the ashes. We've taken the rest of Ms. Anderson's belongings and printed every inch of the room and landing. Sorry about the mess but it's all yours now."

"I can clean it?"

"Yep. You might want to get one of the girls to do that. You're supposed to take it easy for a few days."

"Don't worry," Trout said, "I've got it covered."

Duncan gave him a long assessing look. "Uh, huh." With that he strode across the foyer and out of the Paradise.

Chapter Six

So, Megs and Bartholomew aren't as barmy as I thought. Under the circumstances, I can understand their paranoia to a degree. Though they do take themselves far too seriously, in my opinion. It's not like their lives are in danger or that there's a federal prison for wayward cats. Still, it could be that they would lose their freedom and that's something to be guarded against. A cat is a natural hunter, and the call of the wild still stirs our blood. Fortunately, Dax understands my need for space and freedom. That's why we make such good traveling companions. And, it's why he doesn't fret whenever I get my teeth into a situation. Forget about that old saying that curiosity killed the cat. Not on my watch!

Could sanctions from the government be motive enough to kill? I don't think so. This is Key West in August, after all. It's much too hot and humid to expend the energy necessary to commit murder.

Unless there's a lot better reason than wandering cats. Perhaps it isn't about the cats. Maybe it's about control of … what? The museum? The Hemingway house itself? I'm sure that would be worth a pretty penny. But how would that work to anyone's advantage?

That brings us back to square one. The mystery still remains as to why Liberty had a box full of someone's ashes in her room, and who that someone might be. Maybe that's at the heart of it all. Until we identify the remains we'll never know.

Right, then. It's time I nudged Ginger into action.

* * *

Callahan twined between Ginger's legs as she and Trout watched Duncan pull out of the parking bay of the Paradise.

"What do you think?" Trout asked. "Will he keep us in the loop?"

"Fifty-fifty, I'd say. He's pretty unhappy about the box of ashes. And the cell phone."

"That's the impression I got."

"It's an ego thing, too, I imagine. Duncan does like to be in charge." She realized how that sounded as soon as it was out of her mouth. Trout let it slide.

"So, what do you propose we do?" he asked.

Ginger turned toward the rear of the building. "I saved all of Liberty's photos and call log to my phone. Duncan hasn't had any luck contacting her family, so I suggest we try."

"You sly dog," Trout said. "Who knew you could be so devious."

"It wasn't devious. I need to save my business if that's still possible. This whole dead body, box of unidentified ashes, and guests rousted from their afternoon nap isn't going to do a whole lot for my bottom line." Ginger hoped that the very real fear she was experiencing didn't show in her voice. She didn't want to come across as one those helpless women who fell apart when things got tough. The Paradise wasn't only her business, it was her home and her history. She had to save it.

"I'm surprised by the Talents," Trout said. "You'd think with all this mayhem a young couple celebrating their first anniversary would be falling all over themselves to get away from such macabre happenings."

"I think the operative words are first anniversary." Ginger grinned. "As for Mademoiselle Benoit, she's expecting some kind of business connection and hovers near the phone day and night. And she's French."

"I don't know what being French has to do with anything, but she didn't sit home waiting for the phone to ring last night."

Ginger opened the door to her quarters and sat at her desk. "How do you know?"

"She was still out when you got knocked on the head and she didn't return until shortly after two this afternoon. I got the impression she wasn't out at a business meeting."

"How could you tell?"

"Well," Trout smiled, "she stayed out all night and when she came waltzing in, she had that certain look about her. As you said, she's French."

Ginger laughed. "Men."

"'Tis true, I'm but a mere man, but I've had years of training in observation. I report to you only what I saw and my deductions from it."

"Very noble of you." Ginger booted up her laptop

and took out her cell phone. "Let's start with the numbers Liberty called in the time before she got here. The police have probably checked likely listings in her contacts and the obvious ones like Boss. They may not have gotten around to someone she calls less frequently. Hopefully that someone will answer the phone of an unfamiliar caller from Key West."

"You do that, and I'll look through these photos and see how many local spots I can identify."

Callahan hopped onto Ginger's lap and placed his forepaws on the edge of her desk. "Yeow."

Ginger scratched his ears and said, "Not now."

Trout scrolled through the shots on the phone's camera while Ginger used the landline to dial a number listed under Babs.

"Here's a picture of Jerry," Trout said. "I'm sure he'll remember her. Marilyn is his favorite pin-up."

Ginger clicked the speaker button on the desktop phone.

"Hello?" A female voice answered.

Callahan's ears twitched and Ginger sat forward in her chair. "Hi," she said. "I'm trying to reach a family member of Liberty Anderson."

There was a pause on the other end of the line. "Who's this?"

"My name is Ginger Browne. I own the Paradise Bed and Breakfast in Key West."

"Why are you looking for Liberty?"

"Are you related to Ms. Anderson?"

"No." Another pause. "She's a friend. You said the Paradise? Isn't that where she's staying?"

"Ms. Anderson is a registered guest here. The police

have been trying to reach her family. There's been an accident."

"Oh, dear. Is she in the hospital? Is it serious?"

"Can you tell me why Ms. Anderson came to Key West?"

There was another brief silence. "This is something serious, isn't it? Is Liberty all right?"

"It would be better to get the details from the police. Do you mind telling me your name?" Ginger held her breath hoping the woman wouldn't hang up on her.

"Barbara Delinsky. Liberty and I used to work together. I quit to be a stay-at-home mom."

"And she came to Key West because of work?"

"The Hemingway cats. It's a plum assignment. There's a regular rotation of the field agents so no one gets bent out of shape. Normally it's just a couple of days of fun and sun for routine checks but when there's an actual complaint, whoever is up for the next assignment is guaranteed at least a week in paradise."

"Did she say she was meeting anyone here?"

"No. But I haven't talked to her in at least a couple of months. I only know what's going on from her Facebook page."

Trout was mouthing the word family and Ginger nodded.

"Is there a family member I could call, a husband, mother, or father?"

"No." Another pause. "Her husband left her six months ago. It's been a really bitter legal battle. His name is Arthur. I don't know how to get in touch with him, but I don't imagine he'd be concerned about her accident. They weren't married that long. Less than two years, I think."

"And there's no one else?"

"Not that I'm aware of. She had a lot of friends, but I never thought they were close, you know? More like party friends you see out all the time but not the kind you stay in and watch a movie with or go shopping."

Trout was jotting notes on a pad during the conversation. He wrote BOYFRIEND? in block letters and showed it to Ginger.

"Was she dating, do you know?"

"I couldn't say. All I know of the past few months is what she's posted on Facebook and tweeted. I knew she was on the roster for the next site visit, and when the complaint came in it was naturally assigned to her. That was about two weeks ago. She was thrilled about it. But she hasn't mentioned anyone in particular in her life. Though it might not be something she'd want to plaster all over Facebook right now with the divorce and all." Another pause. "Have you called her boss?"

"I understand the police have talked to him."

"He'll probably be able to tell you who to contact. There should be someone listed in her employment file in case of an emergency."

"Thanks." Ginger looked at Trout and gestured with her hand for any other questions he might have. He shook his head. "I appreciate you speaking with me."

"Is … is Liberty dead?"

"The Key West police department can answer your questions, Mrs. Delinsky. Ask for Detective Moore."

"Oh, my God."

"Thank you, Mrs. Delinsky." Ginger hung up the phone. Her hand was shaking. She looked up at Trout. "I didn't know what to say. I should have realized she would ask."

"You did the right thing." He took her hand in his. "There's no easy way to tell someone about a death. You did great."

"Then why do I feel like a dirty rotten scoundrel for calling that poor woman out of the blue and scaring her like that?"

"She would find out eventually. This way, maybe we can get a jump on a motive. A bad divorce is a good place to start." He turned the laptop around so he could access the keyboard. "Let's see if we can find Arthur Anderson. He's probably living in D.C., or Virginia. We'll start there."

Trout typed the name in the search bar. "Wow. Who knew there could be that many Arthur Andersons."

"Duncan has probably already gotten his name and contact information from her boss."

"Yes, but Duncan isn't sharing." Trout typed some more, and the people finder page showed a less daunting list of names but still more than it would be feasible to contact. "I wonder what Arthur's middle name is."

"Try legal filings. If they're getting a divorce, there should be court records."

"Good idea." Trout typed and clicked across several links then sat back from the computer. "Whoa."

"What?" Ginger looked up from the screen of her phone.

"This doesn't look good." He turned the computer so she could see the display.

"Oh, my God."

* * *

Trout couldn't believe his eyes. There on the computer

screen was a photograph of a man he remembered seeing on Liberty's phone. The problem was, the photo on the computer accompanied an obituary notice. Arthur Langford Anderson died eighteen days ago. Cause of death unspecified. He was survived by his ex-wife, Melissa Harper Anderson, and his current wife, Liberty Nielsen Anderson. The guy had to be ninety if he was a day.

"That explains the box of ashes." Trout looked up at Ginger.

"I bet she was going to spread his ashes in the ocean." Ginger leaned back in her chair. "That's why she chartered your boat."

"Could be. Who writes an obituary listing the ex-wife?"

"The ex-wife."

"Right," Trout said. "Wonder what the cause of death was."

"He was ninety-one."

"That would do it. We need to tell Duncan. "

Ginger picked up her phone and dialed then tapped the speaker button. When Duncan answered she said, "Hey, Trout and I found some information on the ashes."

"Arthur Anderson," Duncan said.

"Right, well, we thought you'd want to know."

"The Key West Police Department isn't totally incompetent, Ginger. We can occasionally find our rear ends if we're allowed to use both hands."

"I wasn't trying to do your job, Duncan. I just want to know what's going on at the Paradise before I lose everything."

There was a brief pause before Duncan said, "You should leave it to me, Ginger. I'll get to the bottom of this. Now that we're pretty certain the ashes belong to Ms.

Anderson's deceased husband, we're back to the date rape overdose scenario. My guys are canvassing all the local hot spots. It's just a matter of time and manpower."

"Great. Thanks."

"I know that tone of voice." Duncan's sigh came through the speaker. "For once don't be so pig-headed."

"Right." She hung up.

Trout had enough sense to keep his mouth shut. Into the silence, Jules called from the nether regions of the bed and breakfast proclaiming he was on the premises and ready for duty.

After a few moments Ginger said. "How's that list coming? Did you identify any of Liberty's watering holes?"

"A few. I've experienced a great many of Key West's bars but not all of them."

"Let's start with what you've got. I can't sit on my hands and wait. If the killer came back for the phone, I want to know. If not, then what did he want?"

"Let's go see if we can find out." Trout saw the fire of determination in Ginger's eyes and knew she wouldn't stop until she had some answers. He wasn't about to let her go on the hunt for a killer on her own. There were a number of iffy places around Key West as there are in any city, not the least of which was the Oriole. It wasn't that far from the marina and he'd been known to frequent it from time to time. It wasn't the kind of place for a woman to be on her own, especially if she was asking difficult questions.

* * *

At last, we're actually going to do something. Surely there will be plenty of people who remember Liberty. Though she was no friend to me, it appears she could be quite charming to humans, particularly male humans.

I spy Megs through the window of Ginger's room. Bartholomew can't be far. The two are inseparable although I think it's purely a platonic relationship considering how uninhibited she is around me. The ladies do love my dense fur and my distinctive ears and I've been told more than once that I have bedroom eyes.

Ah, well, no one can compare to my Veronica so it's back to work for me. Megs and Bartholomew can keep tabs on the Paradise while I accompany Ginger and Trout. They'll need my finely honed skills of deduction, not to mention my keen sense of smell if we encounter our murderer.

The plan is to work through the places captured on Liberty's phone. It would probably be more time efficient if we started at the last place she photographed, but Trout seems to think it would be better to get the full picture and learn how her night progressed. I can't argue with his logic.

There's nothing to distinguish the Green Parrot from any number of other bars in Key West except for a variety of wooden parrots and strings of green lights delineating the seams of what looks like an upside-down multicolored umbrella over the bar. In reality, it's some kind of parachute material. The walls are covered with slogans, paintings, and photographs. And, I do believe those are articles of feminine undergarments. Why, I couldn't say. Talk about airing your dirty laundry!

The bar itself appears to be well-stocked with both alcohol of all sorts and people, also of all sorts. I recognize the pool table as one of the photo props Liberty used.

Trout engages the bartender, a man with no hair on his head but a ferocious mustache. This is the aforementioned Jerry who is enamored of Marilyn, whoever she may be.

"I remember her, all right," *he says with a heavy Aussie*

accent. "She'd be hard to miss, hugging up on all the guys at the bar and generally pissing off all the women."

"Any guy in particular that took a fancy to her?" *Trout asked.*

"I already told the cops. No one was shunning her, but I don't think anyone did more than enjoy the attention."

"Did she leave with anyone?"

"No. She sat at a table with a fat mate in a white linen suit and they had their heads together for a bit but he was still sitting there when she left."

"Did you know the guy?"

Jerry shrugs. "No. He's been in here a few nights, mainly just crowd watching and drinking dark beer. He did like his pint. Another blonde joined him at the table last night and they had their heads together for a good little bit but he didn't leave with her either. I know that for sure."

"Oh?"

Jerry grins but says nothing.

"You don't know who he is?" *Trout asks.*

"Well, he certainly wasn't a conch or a regular either."

"Would you recognize him if you saw him again, you think?"

"Sure."

A patron on the other side of the bar begins clamoring for a drink. As Jerry turns to see to his other customers, he leans back over the bar and says, "Sorry about the dead body, Ginger."

"Thanks, I guess."

"Don't worry, everyone is spreading the word that the Paradise is the best bed and breakfast in town."

Ginger laughs. "Don't oversell it, Jerry. I can't afford any more disappointed guests."

He gives her a brief salute and turns to his customer.

There's nothing to see and no one to question at the zero mile marker for U. S. Highway One so we move on to the next photo op.

Margaritaville is a madhouse of people trying to talk over each other and the music as they drink and wait to be seated for dinner. No one working here remembers seeing Liberty but it's now two days since she passed this way and for most of the waitstaff one tourist looks pretty much like another. I sympathize with their plight.

We have no better luck at Sloppy Joe's and now that we've reached the Chart Room Bar all of us are ready to take a breather and regroup. I confess this is my preferred choice. There are those who would turn their noses up at a hotdog but then they haven't had a hotdog at the Chart Room Bar. If it's good enough for the Rockefellers and Jimmy Buffett, then it's good enough for me. Quite delicious, actually.

It's not crowded here, and the bartender has time on his hands to answer our questions. He tells us he has only just come on duty after being off the previous evening. He confesses that he was about to cut Liberty off when her friends decided to help her back to her hotel that night.

"Did you tell the police this?" *Ginger asks.*

"No. Like I said, I got off at three that morning and haven't been back at work until now. I haven't talked to the cops."

"What did her friends look like?" *Trout wants to know.*

"A young couple. I didn't realize they knew her at first. They came in after her and sat at a table. It was only when she began insisting on another drink that they came over and helped her to her feet."

"How do you know they were her friends?" *Ginger asks.*

"They called her by name, and she seemed to recognize them."

Well, now, here's a clue indeed. Was this some acquaintance she acquired since arriving in Key West, I wonder? Or did someone follow her here from Washington, D.C.?

Trout takes some cash from his pocket and pays for their drinks. "What time was this?" *he asks the bartender.*

"Must have been about one. Something like that. Regulars start to arrive about then, so, yeah, about one."

The bartender takes the money and rings up their drinks.

"Do you think it was the Talents?" *Trout asks Ginger.*

"No. It was about one when Callahan started acting up. I looked to see if Liberty's key was on the hook. I was afraid he was going to wake her. The Talent's key was gone so I knew they were already in for the night."

"We need to identify this couple. This is the first we've heard of her knowing anyone here in Key West." *Trout sits in thought for a minute.* "Did anyone think to ask if this was Liberty's first assignment to check on the Hemingway cats?"

"I don't know."

"Do you have your phone?"

"Yes."

"Let's see if the bartender can identify these friends from the photos you copied from Liberty's phone."

I'm beginning to think Trout has potential. Perhaps his former profession has made him more intuitive than most people.

* * *

Trout watched the bartender scroll through the photos. He shook his head. "Can't help you, man. I don't see them in any of these shots."

"Thanks." Trout handed the phone back to Ginger. "Did it strike you as odd that the couple didn't acknowledge

Liberty when they first entered the bar?"

"Yes. It's possible they didn't see her when they first came in and only became aware of her when she got loud and demanding."

"It's a small bar."

"True." Ginger looked around the room. "Too small, in fact."

"According to what we know, she wasn't exactly hiding her candle under a bushel. So, the question becomes, why didn't they acknowledge her when they came in?"

"Good question. Maybe because she was drunk and they didn't want to get roped into her evening. They could have decided to step in when it looked like she was going to get into trouble."

Trout shelled a peanut and ate it, his focus on the wall behind the bar, his mind chasing something on the edge of his memory. It wouldn't come so he let it go. "What next?"

"Do you think she went to the Oriole? There aren't any pictures from there that I can tell. So much of what she took after here is out of focus and could be any number of bars. Maybe she'd forgotten all about the Oriole, but it almost seems as if she was working her way in that direction. She did ask you about it earlier in the evening."

"I can't see her friends taking her there if she was as drunk as the bartender said."

"Then where did she go? She wasn't at the Paradise."

Trout shook his head. "You hungry?"

"You just ate a hotdog."

"It's way too early to get answers at the Oriole so we might as well get something decent to eat. A hotdog just doesn't cut it for me."

"What then?"

"My place. We're almost there and Sawyer has some snapper from my last catch in his freezer." Trout wasn't sure why the invitation popped out of his mouth. In truth, it was too early to find anyone at the Oriole that would likely have encountered Liberty. The late-night crowd would be the best bet in that endeavor. He supposed the invitation sprang from his need to keep an eye on Ginger, to prevent her wandering into trouble on her own in pursuit of a killer. *Yeah, right*, he thought.

At that moment Ginger's cell phone rang. She looked at the caller ID. "It's the Paradise." She touched the green button on the phone and held it to her ear. "Paradise…" She frowned. "Wait…" She listened. "What do you mean, she wants the ashes?"

Trout had been watching the cat, who had invited himself along on their little jaunt across Key West. Ginger's comment got his full attention and that of the cat. When Trout raised his eyebrows in a questioning look, Ginger shook her head and shrugged.

"Okay, okay. I'm on my way back. Ten minutes. Just tell her to wait."

Ginger ended the call. "You'll never guess who's at the Paradise."

"So, tell me."

"Mel Anderson, as in Melissa Harper Anderson, first ex-wife of Arthur Anderson, who, by the way, is also known as Arty."

"The plot thickens."

"Indeed, it does. She's demanding Jules give her Arty's ashes."

Chapter Seven

Mel Anderson was an older, less endowed version of Liberty. Two vertical lines were permanently etched on her forehead. Her tomato red lips pulled down in a frown. She turned on Ginger the moment she walked through the door of the Paradise.

"Tell this idiot to give me Arty's ashes. I'm the executor of his estate and I have every right to them." She waved a rather battered sheath of papers before Ginger's face.

"And you are?" Ginger asked.

"I've already told this moron. I'm Arty's wife. I'm here to retrieve his ashes. That slut stole them from the mausoleum." Mel's face grew a deeper red as her voice pitched higher. "I'm suing them, too. They should have had security on the premises. But no, not Forest Springs. They don't even have cameras." Her gestures were becoming more out of control as her agitation grew.

Trout stepped forward and said, "You're upset, Mrs. Anderson, and rightfully so. We want to help you resolve the problem. Would you like a cup of tea?"

"Got any gin?" she asked but Trout's words and tone were already having an effect on her.

With a glance, Ginger sent Jules scurrying in the direction of the tiki bar. "Let's move into the sitting room and get comfortable. Jules will bring you something to calm you down."

"As long as it's gin," Mel said.

"I'm sure it will be," Ginger replied. "This way." She made a sweeping gesture with her hand and Mel Anderson preceded them from the foyer. Ginger gave Trout a small smile of thanks; then the two of them trailed behind Mel into the sitting room.

Jules arrived with the gin, placed it on a coaster on the small table beside Mel's chair, and quickly escaped to just beyond the entrance to the room, his ear cocked to, no doubt, capture the conversation that was about to ensue.

Mel took a bracing gulp of gin then stared at Ginger first, then Trout. "Well," she finally said into the silence. "Where are Arty's ashes?"

"The police have them," Ginger said.

"Police? Why would they have them? Don't tell me those idiots in D.C. had them confiscated. They could hardly be bothered to take the report."

"Why do you think Liberty stole them?" Trout asked.

"To deny Arty his last wish."

"What was his last wish?" Ginger asked.

"To have his ashes at Forest Springs next to me. We planned everything, matching urns and all. That piranha was only ever after his money. But she didn't get that either." A malicious smile spread over Mel's face.

"Who did get it?" Ginger asked.

The smile disappeared. "That hasn't been settled yet. She claims he made a new will but he didn't." Tears formed in Mel's eyes. "I know Arty didn't do that to me."

"How did you know where to find Liberty?" Trout's question was softly spoken.

"Facebook, of course. The bitch has been posting pictures for four days. She's having a ball, drinking and partying all across Key West." A tear escaped and trailed down Mel's cheek. "Poor Arty. He was such a fool. He's barely dead and she's sleeping with every man who crosses her path."

"How long were you and Arty married?" Trout asked.

"Ten years." Mel sniffed. "We were happy."

Ginger thought they couldn't have been that happy if Arty divorced her and married Liberty. As to Arty wanting to spend eternity entombed next to Mel, that was also doubtful. Their ten-year marriage also suggested that Arty had married Mel when she was about Liberty's age. She wondered if the latest divorce proceedings had been fueled by yet another Mel/Liberty lookalike. "When did you get here, Mrs. Anderson? Where are you staying?"

"I just got here. Flew into Jacksonville then took a puddle jumper here. Had a four-hour layover. Could have driven it in that amount of time." She took another drink of her gin. "I booked a room at the Pier House before I left Virginia, but I came straight here. I didn't want to risk Liberty skipping town before I got Arty's ashes."

Ginger tried to think like Duncan. How much should she reveal to the grieving ex-widow? "How long are you planning to stay in Key West?" she asked.

"Just tonight. It's too expensive down here and that's coming from someone who lives in spitting distance of the capitol. I thought winter was the height of the season for Key West."

"We really don't have much of an off-season anymore. August isn't our busiest month, for sure, but prices don't fluctuate as much as they once did." Ginger glanced into the foyer, looking for Mel's luggage. "Did you send your bags on to the Pier House?"

"No." Mel lifted a purse the size of a diaper bag. "Since I'm only here to get Arty's ashes, I'm traveling light. Didn't want the bother and fuss of being strip searched at the airport." She drained her glass of the last of the gin. "I'm going to wait right here until that hussy shows up and I'm giving her a piece of my mind."

Ginger shared a look with Trout. "I'm afraid that's not possible."

"You kicking me out?" Mel's expression was turning aggressive again.

"No," Trout interposed. "Liberty isn't coming back to the Paradise."

"Checked out already?"

"No. The police have her."

A smile spread across Mel's face. "Hot damn. Don't tell me they arrested her. For stealing Arty?"

Obviously, the thought that Liberty might have been arrested gave Mel great pleasure. It also reinforced what Ginger had already decided. Mel Anderson didn't know what had happened to Liberty.

"She's at the morgue, Mrs. Anderson. She's dead."

* * *

Detective Moore sent a patrol car to pick up a very gleeful Mel Anderson. If her story hadn't been so unbelievable, I would consider her our number one suspect. But, as they say, truth is stranger than fiction. No one is likely to pronounce their undying hatred of a murder victim unless they know they're in the clear. The good news is that the ashes have been dealt with and we can get on to the matter at hand. Unless there's another ex-Mrs. Anderson lurking out there somewhere, we still have no idea why Liberty was murdered.

Ginger and Trout are in the kitchen together cooking up some heavenly smelling dish of shrimp in a sauce, over wild rice. A bottle of wine is breathing on the worktable. The conversation has moved away from dead bodies, ex-wives, and poison.

I feel very much a third wheel. If I wasn't so famished, I'd give them their privacy. But, at last dinner is served. Not only is Ginger a fine pastry chef, she's a whiz at quick, easy, gourmet dishes that would thrill the soul of Gordon Ramsey. Not that I've ever had a chance to sample any of his dishes, but Trudy the Tour Guide from Warm Springs kept the television tuned to the cooking network. She was quite smitten with him. Even to the point of taking a vacation in New York City just to eat at one of his restaurants. And if Trudy says he's the best, then he's the measuring stick by which I judge all chefs. If I ever get the chance.

I'm stuffed, having eaten every last morsel of shrimp. Now, I'll take myself off before the kitchen gets any hotter. I've never seen two adults dance around their attraction for each other so much.

There's no sign of Megs or Bartholomew. I suspect they—What's that I smell? I do believe it's our killer. Where is it coming from?

I put my nose to the air and I'm off. He has the gall to return to the scene of the crime a third time. Yes, he stood here in the shadow of this mahogany tree, spying on the Paradise.

Let's see where his scent takes us. If only I could risk the time it would take to alert Ginger and Trout, but I can't risk losing his trail. Never mind. I'll find and identify him. Justice for Liberty is only a matter of time now.

* * *

Ginger felt flushed from the heat of the kitchen. That's what she told herself anyway. An evening that started out as a search for a killer had turned into an intimate dinner in the kitchen of the Paradise. She was feeling the wine, but she was also feeling the attraction of a handsome man, one she had been drawn to for months. No more wine she told herself; then he opened the fridge and took out another bottle.

"Why don't we take this out by the pool; what do you say?"

"Yes. That would be nice. It's too hot in here."

Trout worked the corkscrew then caught up their two glasses and headed for the back door.

Ginger took off her apron, ran her fingers through her hair, and told herself to keep things platonic. She had enough problems at the moment and didn't need to add the uncertainty and demands that a relationship would throw into the mix.

For a late August night, it was surprisingly cool. At least it was cooler than the kitchen. The up-lights in the palm trees and the glimmer of the pool lights made a lovely setting for a couple ending a busy day in paradise.

It occurred to Ginger how rarely she took advantage of her home and its amenities. It felt good to lie back in an outdoor lounge chair and sip the oaky chardonnay. She resolved, in that moment, to do this more often.

Trout sighed and took a sip of his wine. "This is the life."

A response about the long hours and hard work was on the tip of Ginger's tongue but she stopped herself in time. She wanted to enjoy the moment, to be simply a guest in her own establishment, enjoying a glass of wine, and the company of a handsome man. "Yes," she said. "It is."

"How long have you run the bed and breakfast?"

"Always. Well, my grandmother ran it, then my mother. I've lived and worked here my whole life. I inherited it three years ago."

"You're a native, then."

"A true conch of the Republic."

"That's nice. Belonging is important."

Ginger thought she heard a hint of longing in his voice. She let the silence settle around them. All was quiet except for the distant voices of people on the street and a faint thread of music drifting on the night air. It was a comfortable, intimate bubble of companionship. After a time, she asked, "Do you miss your old life?"

Trout didn't answer immediately. Finally, he said, "It's hard to know what I feel. Sometimes I have guilt about bailing when I know there are so many kids who need help." The quiet returned and they sat amiably sipping their wine.

Trout cleared his throat. "I couldn't do it anymore. Not after Missy's death. She left a note." After a long pause he said, "'I told you I wanted to die, Dr. Richardson.' That's what she wrote."

"Oh, Trout. I'm sorry."

"Yeah, well, me too. But not for myself, for that scared

little girl who had nowhere to turn. No one to protect her. She simply couldn't live with her demons any longer." He drank down the last of his wine, leaned his head against the cushion of the lounge chair, and closed his eyes.

Ginger felt the sting of tears and knew she couldn't trust herself to speak. Her throat was tight with grief for a troubled young girl and for the man who tormented himself with the knowledge he couldn't save her.

* * *

The evening had been going so well, Trout thought. Over the course of the meal Ginger had let go of her worry about the fate of the Paradise. It was just as well that she brought up his former life. Trout had let down his guard. Her nearness did that to him. He couldn't afford to let Ginger into his life. Her or anyone. It was just too painful to care.

He wanted to pour another glass of wine but didn't want her to see him in a bad way. He lay there on the lounger with his eyes closed trying to decide how long he should stay. She would feel bad about bringing up the topic of his former life if he left immediately. He didn't want to ever do anything to make her feel bad. As Duncan had said, she was good people.

A rustling sounded in the staghorn ferns. Trout opened his eyes to see a really fat cat waddle from the low foliage surrounding one of the palm trees. It was soon followed by a much smaller cat. They stopped and stared at him and Ginger, then carried on across the patio, onto the back porch, and up the stairs leading up the outside of the building to the second floor.

"Where'd they come from?" he asked, glad for something to distract from their earlier conversation.

"Hemingway cats. That's Lou Costello and Mitzi Gaynor."

"With crossed eyes?"

"I guess they didn't realize her eyes would be that way when they named her. And I don't know of any Hollywood actress with crossed eyes so whoever she was named after was going to be an imperfect fit."

"Why not give her a different name, then?"

"Tradition. All the Hemingway cats are named for Hollywood stars."

"I should probably do the tour."

"It's interesting," Ginger said. "It brings a lot of tourists. That and Mel Fisher's Museum."

They were making small talk, trying to get past the awkwardness of his earlier confession, Trout realized. He was forming the words of an excuse to leave in his mind when a woman's scream pierced the night.

Trout and Ginger jumped to their feet and looked toward the bed and breakfast. The front door of the Paradise banged open against the outer wall and a slim figure dressed in black went flying down the front steps. Trout took off after the fleeing man.

* * *

The scent has brought me to Mallory Square. The culprit is up ahead somewhere. Ah, what's this? A fat man sitting on an iron bench looking out over the water. He's the source of the scent. He reeks of it. How can this be? Whoever knocked Ginger unconscious was slender and agile. She remembers him fleeing quickly down the stairs. *The man before me could hardly walk down a flight of stairs much less run down them.*

I have no choice but to use the oldest of the tried-and-true methods of a gumshoe: a stakeout. This man is involved in the happenings at the Paradise. Could he be the man Liberty talked with at the Green Parrot? He certainly fits Jerry's description, right down to the white linen suit.

He's checking his watch. Our suspect is waiting for someone. I'll wait with him. He's oblivious of my presence. With so many cats on the island, I'm just one of many. This will be a piece of cake. I'll just move closer so I can hear his conversation when his accomplice arrives.

"Hello, cat," *Fat Man says.* "Haven't I seen you somewhere before?"

I ignore him. It's a good thing cats are known for being rude and indifferent. Surely, he can't suspect that I'm a super sleuth hot on his trail.

"I know where I've seen you. The Paradise."

I move beyond him and under a nearby tree. A flock of chickens squawks and flaps their wings. I've disturbed them in their roosting place. Whatever possessed the good citizens of Key West to allow chickens to roam the streets at will? I slink away under the shadow of the tree, and they begin to settle. I make my way back to Fat Man on the bench but this time I'm behind him.

From his movements I can tell he's checking his watch again. He sighs heavily. "Where are they?" *he mumbles.*

Time crawls by. The pedestrian traffic along Mallory Square has died away to an occasional tourist. Fat Man sighs again and starts the process of shifting his immense weight from the bench. Just as he has managed some momentum, a couple comes hurrying toward him. I recognize them immediately.

"Well?" *Fat Man says.*

"Nothing," *Mr. Talent says.*

"Nothing?"

"She must have it somewhere else." *Mrs. Talent's voice holds a note of apology.*

"Hmmm." *Fat Man heaves himself to his feet.* "This bears some thought. Where could she keep it if not in her room? Does the Paradise have a safe?"

"Yes, but there's nothing in it." *Mr. Talent looks down and sees me.* "Isn't that the odd looking cat from the Paradise?"

Fat Man turns and sees me. "Yes. He followed me here earlier."

Odd looking? Really! My cover is blown but I see no reason for concern. They can't possibly know I'm on to them.

"Forget the cat, Ray," *Mrs. Talent says.* "What are we going to do?"

"I have something in mind," *Fat Man says.* "I'll have to think through the details. Wait until you hear from me." *With that he turns and heads back along the square at an ambling pace.*

I'm torn as to who to follow and decide it's best to know as much as possible about Fat Man. The Talents will be at the Paradise. I can find out what they're up to later. For now, I'm tailing Fat Man.

What could he be after? It certainly isn't Arty's ashes. Ginger and Trout thoroughly searched the Toucan Suite as did the Key West police department. Twice. There wasn't a hint of what could be at stake. Whatever it is, at least I now know that it would fit into the safe of the Paradise.

We continue along Wall Street, Fat Man in no particular hurry. I assume that's because his weight prevents him from having a second gear. I confess that surveillance isn't my favorite activity but then he stops and I'm encouraged.

He stares into the window of a shop. The sign bears the image of a fat cigar with a thin trail of smoke rising from it. Fat Man searches the inner pocket of his white linen jacket, then tries the door. It's locked at this late hour. Fat Man sighs and moves along. I foresee a long night ahead of me.

Chapter Eight

Whoever ran from the screaming Annette Benoit and the Paradise was fast and knew the lay of the land much better than Trout. Within two blocks he had lost his prey. Checking dark driveways and dense foliage only got him barking dogs. When he got back to the bed and breakfast, Ginger was refilling Annette's snifter with brandy.

Ginger looked up as he came through the door. "Anything?"

He shook his head. "What happened, Ms. Benoit?"

"Someone was in my room." She pushed a heavy wave of blond curls back from her forehead. Her face was pale, but she wasn't the weepy, hysterical type. "I opened the door, and he shoved right past me." She took a drink of the brandy. "I screamed."

"Did you get a look at him?"

"No." She gestured with her hand, a downward motion from her forehead to her chin. "He wore, how do you say in English, ... over the face."

"A ski mask."

"No, no. It was ... how you say ... funny ... like, um, clown." She looked from Trout to Ginger and back again. "How did he get into my room? The key was on the hook when I came back to the hotel." She took another sip of brandy then said, "How did he get in?" It was less a question this time and more a matter of puzzlement.

Trout and Ginger exchanged a look. How indeed did someone get into the Bird Cage without the key. Ginger went behind the desk, opened the top drawer and held up the ring of master keys.

"Can you think of any reason someone would want to break into your room? Did you leave jewelry, money there? Your passport?" Trout asked.

"No. I do not bring fine jewelry when I travel. And my money and passport are with me." She gestured toward her purse on the seat of the sofa.

"There was nothing else of value anyone would want?"

A spark of something flashed across Annette's features but was so quickly gone that Trout couldn't be sure he had seen it. She averted her eyes, shook her head, and fiddled with the glass of brandy, turning it round and round in her hands.

"How did he get in?" She glanced up at Ginger. "If I hadn't broken the heel of my shoe, he would have come and gone, and no one would have known."

"I don't know," Ginger said, "but I intend to find out. Jules was supposed to be on the desk tonight. There's no sign of him." She took out her cell phone and dialed his number. A muffled voice saying 'It's the boss, pick up the phone. It's the boss, pick up the phone,' could be heard.

Ginger lowered the phone and turned in the direction of the voice. "That's Jules' ring tone." She took off toward the kitchen. The pantry door stood partially open. Coffee grounds were scattered all over the floor of the pantry and out into the kitchen. The soles of Jules' high tops were clearly visible. Ginger stepped over his sprawled legs and knelt beside his inert body. "Oh, my God."

Trout was on her heels. He felt the artery in Jules' neck. "He has a pulse." Then he gently moved Jules' head enough to see the deep bloody gash on his forehead. "Call Duncan and an ambulance."

He helped Ginger back across Jules' legs and took out his phone. After he snapped several photos of the pantry and Jules' from different angles, he opened a kitchen drawer and found a clean cloth. He held it to Jules' wound and the young man moaned.

* * *

"I gotta tell ya, Ginger, you're keeping me up nights, and not in a good way." Duncan said, as he surveyed the kitchen and pantry floor. "Why would he be in here?"

"He was probably doing the set-up for breakfast."

"Umm. That's the routine?"

"Yes."

"The intruder must have come in the back door. Otherwise, there would be no need to bash the kid's brains out."

"Really, Duncan."

"Sorry. He'll be okay. He couldn't have been out long if the French dame screamed and you and Romeo came running."

Ginger ignored Duncan's little dig at Trout. "It was at least fifteen minutes, maybe twenty."

"How so?"

"Well, he would have to knock Jules out, take the key and go upstairs, unlock the door to the Bird Cage—"

"Where'd you get all those crazy names for the rooms?"

"My grandmother." Ginger gave him a look that said don't go there. "Anyway, he'd have to bring the key back down—"

"Why?"

"Because Ms. Benoit said the key was on the hook when she came back to the Paradise because of her broken heel."

"Doesn't make sense."

"Will you let me finish?"

"Sure, sure."

"He'd have to return the key, go back upstairs to the room, and be there when Ms. Benoit came in and surprised him. He pushed past her, she screamed, Trout took off after the intruder, and I came through the kitchen to the foyer and found her at the top of the stairs."

"You didn't see the kid in the pantry when you came in the back door?"

"No. It's off to the side as you can see, and the back door lines up with the one into the dining room. I ran straight through. It never occurred to me to look."

"So, the boat captain takes off—"

"His name is Trout."

"He takes off after the intruder, you go to the aid of

your guest. Then what?"

"Ten or fifteen minutes later Trout's back. He lost the guy. We were trying to determine from Ms. Benoit if she had anything that would be the target of a burglar. The problem, as you observed, with how the man got into her room, made me remember that Jules should have been on the desk. I called his phone and that's how we found him, by following the ring tone."

Duncan stared off into space for several seconds. Finally, he sighed and said, "First a woman dies from alcohol and GHB. She's in a locked room. Everything locked up tight. No way for anyone to have been in there with her. Now we have a woman return to the B & B to find a thief rummaging through her things in a room that's locked, the key on the board. How's that possible?"

"You're the detective."

He nodded. "Right. Tell me again why you didn't see whoever it was coming in the back door?"

"We were out by the pool. Our backs were to the main building." Ginger felt the blush creeping up her throat.

Duncan watched her a long moment and nodded again. "Right." He turned toward the door into the hallway, stopped, and looked back at her. "Where is he now?"

"He went to the hospital with Jules. He said he'd stay with him until his mother got there."

"I'll talk to the Benoit woman. Looks like you could use a cup of coffee. Or tea."

"I'm fine."

"Quit worrying so much."

She nodded. Easier said than done, she thought. It was almost as if someone had it in for her and her business. She frowned. No, that couldn't be it. Sawyer Daniels, Trout's friend and sometimes employer with the vintage boat, wanted to buy the Paradise but that didn't have anything to do with what was happening. Sawyer, a fellow conch and lifelong acquaintance, knew she would never sell, and it was more a joke between them than any real intent on his part. There was no one who would benefit if the Paradise closed its doors.

Ginger gave herself a good mental shake and went about the business of tidying up the coffee from the floor of the pantry and the kitchen. The police had dusted the door and anything the intruder might have touched. She took a bucket of warm soapy water and began scrubbing away the mess they left. There would still need to be breakfast for Annette Benoit and the Talents.

Duncan stuck his head around the door of the kitchen when she was cutting fruit for the next morning. "I've done all I can. Too many guests, too many prints for what we've collected to be of much value, but we'll run them and see if we get any hits. Give me a call if you need me."

"Sure. Thanks, Duncan."

He nodded and left.

Ginger finished the breakfast preparations, locked the back door, and turned out the kitchen lights. She fluffed pillows on furniture, picked up Annette's empty brandy snifter, and generally tidied the foyer and sitting room. At the reception desk, she glanced at the key board and straightened the notepad, pens, and credit card machine. Her hand stilled as she dropped the ring of master keys into the drawer. She looked back at the key board. The Talents' key wasn't on its hook.

Surely, they hadn't been so involved in each other that they had been unaware of the break-in and the police all over the place. Again.

"Yeow!" Callahan called from the front porch. His forepaws appeared and disappeared several times just above the wood that formed the bottom panel of the beveled glass door as he scratched at it to get her attention. Ginger sighed. "Darn cat." She unlocked it and let him in. "Where the devil have you been? You need to quit wandering the streets before you get lost. I don't have time for your foolishness."

The cat ignored her and shot up the stairs to the second landing. At the top he turned and looked down at her. "Yeow!"

Ginger followed after him and saw that for once he wasn't obsessing about the Toucan Suite. He went straight to the Talents' room.

Chapter Nine

*G*inger is reluctant to follow me upstairs. I have to make her see that the Talents aren't what they appear to be. I blame myself, of course. Shoddy work on my part, I confess. The notion that there was only one person involved in this business led me to completely discount them.

Finally, Ginger's beginning to realize that something is amiss. She knocks on the door of the Macaw Suite. There's no answer. She knocks again and calls out, "Mr. Talent, Mrs. Talent? Are you in there?"

Silence.

She looks down at me.

"Yeow."

"Right." *She rushes downstairs and returns with the master keys. Once again, she knocks and says,* "Ray, I'm coming in."

The bed is made, and the towels stacked in the bathroom are neat and tidy. A lipstick and some foundation are on the dressing table as is a notepad with some figures on it. One of the Paradise's lush bathrobes is draped across the easy chair, another one on the foot of the bed. Otherwise, the room looks little used.

Across the room, one of the floor-to-ceiling windows onto the gallery is open and the room is quite warm. If a murder on the premises doesn't kill business, then the power bill will. Poor Ginger, the cards are definitely not falling in her favor.

I investigate the room, checking the armoire, highboy, and the bathroom. At the threshold of the window onto the balcony, I discover the strong scent of both Talents. They have traversed this way many times. What is it out here that is such an attraction?

The lounge chairs and table on this end of the gallery are covered in a layer of pollen. No one has been sitting out here. Ray Talent's scent is present, as is that of his wife, but it's faint. It's the path to and from the other end of this lovely covered outdoor space that holds their scent more strongly. The Talents seem to have been intensely interested in the Toucan Suite.

Ginger follows my lead and stands before one of the windows into the Toucan Suite. Tentatively she places a finger under the check rail and pushes. The bottom panel of the double hung window glides upward with a familiar squeak.

The sound of a car door closing draws us to the railing of the gallery. We see a taxi pulling away from the bed and breakfast and Trout coming up the front walk.

* * *

Trout looked up at the sound of Ginger calling his name.

"Up here," she said.

She was waiting on the upstairs landing when he topped the stairs. The door to the Toucan Suite stood open as did the door to the room on the other end of the front-facing hallway.

"I've got something interesting to show you." She led the way to the end room. "This is the Macaw Suite," she said. "The Talents' room."

She walked through the door, over to the windows, and out onto the gallery. She looked back to see that he was following her. "The window was open like this when I came up here a few minutes ago."

With that, she crossed the gallery to the windows opening from the Toucan Suite. The window stood open. "It wasn't locked when I tried it just now but the door to this room was."

"You think the Talents have been using the gallery to get into Liberty's room?"

"The cat thinks so."

Trout looked down at Callahan who sat on his haunches on the gallery floor and watched him with his steady golden gaze. "The cat showed you this?"

Ginger hesitated. "Well, sort of." She blushed. "I had just realized that the Talents hadn't made an appearance all through the investigation of the attack on Annette. I mean, no one could have slept through all that commotion, you know? And I assume the police knocked on their door to see if they heard or saw anything. I don't know for sure, but either way, they weren't here."

"Maybe they didn't want to get drawn into another incident. How can you know with certainty that they weren't here?"

"The key. It wasn't on the board. Which means they

should have been in their room. That's how I know whether all my guests are in or not. They aren't supposed to leave the premises with the key."

"Maybe they forgot. It could have been unintentional."

"It's big and heavy with a large emblem on the ring. You would notice that much bulk and weight in your pocket."

"But maybe not so much a woman's purse," Trout suggested.

Ginger didn't seem convinced. "Maybe. But what about the window to the Toucan Suite? It was locked when we tried it."

"I remember."

"That was after I came home from the hospital. They had hours. The Talents could have been fast and loose with the room keys. At almost any time, really, even before Liberty died. They could have looked for whatever it is that started this whole thing in motion since the day she checked in."

"Wouldn't that be a big risk? What if Liberty came back to her room when they were in there?"

Ginger considered that for a moment. "There are two of them. One could be tailing her while the other searched the room."

"I suppose."

They stared at the open window as if it would give them the answer.

"It would be tricky." Trout said. "Either you or Jules could have caught them out."

"True. Or Angela. But this is a lean operation. All of us wear a multitude of hats. Anyone paying attention would see that they had plenty of opportunity."

"And they'd have access to all the room keys."

Trout saw the look of dismay his comment caused. "It's not your fault, Ginger. We don't even know they had anything to do with her death. Or that they were ever in this room. Duncan's team was in here just hours ago. They could have left the window unlocked."

"Oh, my stars," Ginger said, "I didn't even ask about Jules."

"He's fine. I left him with his mother clucking around him as he posted photos of his bandaged head on Snapchat."

That made Ginger smile. Trout thought she had a beautiful smile. It engaged her whole face, especially her eyes.

"Jules will milk this for all he's worth," she said.

"We'll get him a case of orange Jello."

"Orange?"

"That seems to be his favorite."

Ginger's smile faded. "Oh, Trout, what am I going to do? This has to stop. What if this maniac had killed Jules?"

Trout took her in his arms in a loose embrace. She relaxed against his chest. "We'll find whoever's behind this," he said.

"And if we don't? If the Paradise ends up on the Ghosts and Gravestones tour, the B & B where people go to die?" She leaned her head back to look him in the eye.

"Well," he said, "I guess I'll have to hire you to crew on the *Baby Buddha*."

She laughed and buried her face in his chest.

"Look on the bright side. All this skullduggery does lend itself to some catchy promotions. I'm sure Jules could come up with any number of slogans. *On your way to paradise? Check out at the Paradise.*"

He felt as well as heard Ginger's muffled laughter against his chest. They stood that way for a couple of minutes. Trout knew the moment she became self-conscious. He released her from the embrace as she pulled away.

"What now?" she asked.

"You should call it a night. I'll man the desk. I'm curious to see what the Talents have to say for themselves."

"I can't ask you to spend another sleepless night on my behalf." The brief respite from worry was fading from her features.

"What are friends for, right?"

"But—"

"No buts. Jules isn't the only one with a lump on the head."

"Trout—"

"I wouldn't sleep anyway. Curiosity killed the cat, you know." He shot Callahan a glance and could have sworn the cat gave him a look of disdain.

* * *

Ginger gave in to Trout's insistence that she leave him in charge. She couldn't convince him that all his efforts would be wasted because she was too wired to sleep. Maybe it was because she was so wired that she gave in. Usually, she was calm and in control. This internal turmoil was new to her. Now, in her bed in her pajamas, she tossed and turned.

After twenty minutes, she gave up and went to her desk to make a list. It was one of the tricks she had learned from her grandmother. When the demands of the day wouldn't let go, write them down, then rewrite the list by priority.

Doing so freed the mind of fear that something important would be forgotten. This wasn't exactly a list of things that needed to be done but hopefully, the process would have the same effect.

She decided to write down everything that happened from the time Liberty Anderson checked into the Paradise. First, she noted the guests in the Flamingo Suite were already on the premises, having checked in two days earlier. Another couple had one of the cottages near the pool.

Liberty arrived late Monday afternoon. The room overlooking the pool and the gardens didn't suit her. She wanted one of the more spacious rooms on the front of the bed and breakfast. Since she was willing to pay the higher rate, Ginger switched her to the empty Toucan Suite. As soon as Liberty checked in and deposited her bags in her room, she had gone out.

The Talents, Ray and Crissy, arrived at just about nine on Tuesday morning. Ginger sat back in her chair and tapped the notebook with her pen. Why hadn't she realized this before? Now she saw their arrival so soon after Liberty checked in as suspicious.

She gave herself a mental shake. No jumping to conclusions, she told herself. At this point it was all circumstantial. State the facts, she told herself, and see where they lead.

* * *

I'm glad Trout insisted on manning the front desk tonight. I suspect Ginger could hold her own in most circumstances but we're dealing with a murderer. The Talents have some explaining to do about their involvement in whatever it is that's going on at the

Paradise. The problem is, will Trout know which questions to ask?

My night hasn't been a total waste. I was able to gather some information by tailing Fat Man. First off, his name is Fortesque. Secondly, he's staying at the Curry Mansion Inn. That means he has money to burn. He likes pear brandy for a late-night cordial. And the staff all have a frightened look on their faces when he sits in one of the wicker settees on the verandah.

None of this tells me anything about the object he's pursuing but at least I know where to find him should the need arise.

Well, it's been a busy night. I confess to being rather foot sore. I might as well settle in for a nap until the wayward guests in the Macaw Suite decide to return. Trout is, at the moment, alert and on the job. A smart cat always naps when the opportunity presents itself.

* * *

Trout yawned and stretched. He had weathered the night by burying his nose in *The Guards*, a novel by Ken Bruen. The writing was good and it kept him turning the pages. He hadn't trusted himself to take advantage of the day bed in the small cubby behind the reception desk. Two nights without sleep made the desire to drowse too strong. So, he had ousted the cat from the comfy chair in the foyer and stretched his long legs before him and read until the sun came up. The Talents hadn't returned to the Paradise.

He wandered into the kitchen. The coffee pot was set to go so he flipped the switch and watched until it finished gurgling and hissing. With a cup in hand, he strolled through the downstairs of the bed and breakfast. All was quiet. Even the cat had abandoned him.

When he had finished his coffee, Ginger came through from the kitchen with a small coffee carafe and a plate loaded with fruit and fresh pastries. "Thanks for starting the coffee," she said. "Hungry?" she asked as she refilled his cup.

"Starved."

She placed the plate on a table for two in the bay window of the dining room and went back through to the kitchen. When she returned, she had another plate, napkins, and silverware. "There's orange juice, if you like."

"Thanks. This is great." He sat down in the chair that gave him a view of the side and front lawn of the Paradise and slathered a scone with butter. "No luck last night. The Talents didn't return to the nest."

"You think they're not coming back?"

"Can't say. All they left in the room was make-up, toothbrushes, and a few articles of clothing, not even a complete change for either of them. Not a big loss for most people." He took a drink of his coffee. "I can't see how they fit into the equation. But if they are involved, why wouldn't they return unless they've found what they were searching for?"

"Maybe they know we're on to them."

"That's just it. Are we on to them? Are they involved?"

"I think they are." Ginger took the list she made the night before from her back pocket. "I couldn't sleep so I made a timeline of events since Liberty registered. Ray and Crissy Talent arrived in the early morning after she checked in the previous afternoon. There were no flights arriving at the airport until eleven."

"Maybe they came by car."

"No. Taxi." Ginger ate the mango on her plate.

"Okay. We should check the address they gave when they registered. And their credit card."

"I already did. The address is for a drugstore in Nashville. They paid cash for their room. Five nights in advance. They're good for one more night."

"No credit card?"

"Yes, there's a credit card. The world can't function without a credit card in this day and age. I scanned it against damages or bar charges."

"But?"

"I can't access their financial information. The police would have to do something like that."

"They might still show up. It could be they partied all night in a bar and will come dragging in later."

"Do you think that?" Ginger asked.

"Not really. The false address clinches it. The only problem is we don't know why they were surveilling Liberty."

"Back to square one."

Trout nodded and then dug into the food on his plate. He was hungry, tired, and not feeling particularly sharp this morning.

"I'm going to be off in a few minutes," Ginger said. "They're releasing Jules from the hospital and neither he nor his mother has a car. I need to do some shopping for incoming guests on Wednesday as well." She hesitated. "I hate to ask, but could you man the fort until I get back? It won't take long. Angela will be here soon, but I can't leave her alone under the circumstances."

"Sure. I planned to hang around a while anyway, just to see if the Talents do show up."

"Thanks. I'll be as quick as I can."

Angela had arrived at some point while they ate. She came through from the kitchen and poured him another cup of coffee. Ginger shook her head to a second cup and took her plate to the kitchen.

Trout sipped coffee and looked down Ginger's timetable. Tuesday, Liberty Anderson arrived. Wednesday, Ray and Crissy Talent checked in about nine in the morning. Wednesday afternoon, Annette Benoit had a late arrival due to flight delays. Liberty died some time Thursday night. Ginger surprised the intruder on Friday night. Annette found the intruder in her room on Saturday night. He put the sheet of paper on the table, closed his eyes, and let his mind float.

The sound of someone clearing his throat woke Trout from a light snooze. He looked up to see a man of medium height and weight standing beside his table. He looked to be Hispanic, possibly Cuban, Trout thought. He straightened in his chair. "Can I help you?"

"I'm sorry to disturb you," the man said, "but there seems to be no one about. I'm looking for Ms. Benoit. Would you know her?"

"Yes. She's a guest here. Is she expecting you?"

"Yes and no. We were to meet up for a business transaction, but we seem to have gotten our wires crossed. I thought I'd just pop around and speak with her."

"You're local?"

"Yes."

When no other information was offered, Trout stood and said, "I don't know if Ms. Benoit is in her room."

"Can you tell me which room she's in?"

"How about I call and see if she's in and if she wants to come down to meet with you?"

"You work here?"

"Not officially. Just helping out this morning." Trout

went into the foyer and to the reception desk. He glanced at the key board, picked up the phone, and rang the Bird Cage. After a number of rings with no answer, he frowned and returned the phone to the receiver. "She must have gone out already."

"I see," the man said. He studied Trout for a moment then said. "Perhaps I'll have better luck later."

"Can I give her a message, say who came calling?"

"That's not necessary." The man smiled, crossed the foyer, and went out the door.

Trout returned to the dining room and watched through the windows as the man turned left on the sidewalk and walked away. He hadn't arrived by car, then. A memory stirred in his tired brain. Something Jules had said about Annette Benoit anxiously awaiting a phone call. Was this the mysterious caller she wanted so desperately to hear from? And why wouldn't he reveal his name?

* * *

As Ginger stored the shopping items in the refrigerator and pantry, Callahan came sauntering in through the back door, asking to be fed.

"Why should I?" she asked him. "If you'd been here earlier, you'd have gotten a hot breakfast."

Callahan just looked at her and blinked.

"Right," she said. "Let's see if I remembered cat food."

The cat flicked his scarred right ear and turned his head to the side in a look of longsuffering.

Ginger laughed. "You're funny, you know that? Let's see what I have."

She broke up a scone and added a dollop of strawberry

jam, then a dollop of clotted cream. "That should do you," she said, as she placed the concoction in his bowl on the small mat designated as Callahan's food station. "Bon Appetit."

Callahan gave the dish a sniff then began to eat.

"Where have you been, I wonder?" Ginger said as she opened a recipe file and began flipping through the worn and stained cards. "The Paradise is suddenly overrun with cats. Lou Costello and Mitzi Gaynor are hanging around here a lot more than usual. I think they want you to come out and play."

Callahan gave a violent flick of his tail and looked up at Ginger, ears flattened.

"You really should stay closer to the bed and breakfast. Something could happen to you. Then where would I be, huh? Dax is busy hammering away in the garage apartment this morning. Does he even know where you are? Where you go? I doubt it. So be smart and stop wandering off."

"Who're you talking to?" Trout asked as he came into the kitchen.

Ginger felt her face grow hot. "Myself. Trying to decide on something different for afternoon tea. I like to provide enough finger food so my guests can skip either lunch or dinner if they want. It's so expensive to eat out all the time." She laid the card aside, and leaned against the worktable, supporting her upper body with her forearms. "I get tired of making the same old things and though they're new to my guests, well, I just guess I'm unsettled right now. Looking for something to keep me busy."

"When did you get back?"

"A few minutes ago. I've been putting away the food. And feeding the cat."

"How's Jules?"

"He says he feels fine. Not even a headache, but I doubt that. He wants to come back to work but the doctor said he should take it easy for at least three days. He needed twelve stitches."

"Ouch."

"Yeah, tell me about it."

"What did the intruder hit him with?"

Ginger nodded toward a rack of open shelves. "One of the tall pepper mills. It was the sharp corner of the base that did the damage. They found it in the pantry where the attacker threw it under the shelves used for all the table linens."

"Will he be able to return in time to help with the convention crowd?"

"I can't let him, even though he needs the paycheck. As you know, everything in Key West is expensive. He helps support his mom. This will be a hardship on them. She works as a maid at the Curry Mansion Inn."

"Yeow! Yeow!"

"What the devil…" Trout looked over at the cat presiding over an empty food bowl.

"Who knows," Ginger said. "He's probably still hungry. I suspect he's been out tom catting all night."

"Isn't he, you know, fixed?" Trout asked.

Ginger's voice dropped to a whisper. "Yes. Still, the streets are full of cats and, well, who knows. What nature intended and all that."

She glanced up at Trout and saw he was watching her, a wicked grin on his face. She felt the heat crawling up her throat. Why in the world had she said that? "Any news from Duncan, about the prints?" she asked as she picked up the recipe card and studied it.

"If he had any news, he wouldn't be calling me."

She heard the humor in his voice and sighed. They were both well past the blushing teenage years. She looked him in the eye, shook her head, and smiled in return. "Grow up already."

"I feel all grown up at the moment."

"You're just sleep deprived."

"Is that what it is?"

Ginger found she couldn't hold his gaze any longer, so she turned and picked up Callahan's empty bowl and took it to the kitchen sink. He began to twine between her legs and kept talking as if he needed to impart something to her.

"Are you still hungry?" she asked.

Callahan sat, looked down at the floor, then at her, and finally at Trout. With that he headed to the back door. He sat there, facing the door, his back to them as if giving them the brush off.

"Fine." Ginger crossed the kitchen and opened the door. "Stay close," she said to his disappearing back. She returned to the worktable. "If something happens to him, I'm dead."

"Don't worry, he's a smart cat. And, he has nine lives. Besides, cats are lucky, didn't I tell you? Especially on and around the water."

"If that's true, why don't I feel lucky?"

Trout had no answer for that.

"Well," she said, "I guess I need to clean the Macaw Suite. Even if the Talents are coming back." She looked up at Trout. "No sign of them while I was gone, huh?"

"No," he said, "but something curious happened."

"What?"

"A man came looking for Annette Benoit."

"What's so curious about that?"

"I'm not sure exactly." Trout walked over to the windows overlooking the back patio and pool. "Something about it seemed off, you know?"

"Off how?"

Trout glanced from the view to Ginger with a sheepish expression on his face. "I fell asleep in my chair. I was still in the dining room. Don't know how long I was out but it couldn't have been more than a few minutes. And I woke up to find him standing over me."

"You've had a long couple of nights."

"He said he had a business meeting with Ms. Benoit but that they kept missing each other."

"She's been obsessed about messages. When she goes out for any reason that's her first concern when she returns. Did anyone call."

"It wasn't that, exactly. He wanted to know which room she was in."

"You didn't tell him, did you?"

"No. Especially after the intruder in her room last night. If he didn't know already, then he wasn't going to find out from me. And to be truthful, the fact that he asked didn't bother me at first. It seemed like the kind of question anyone would ask, you know. Like, hi, I'm looking for Dr. Doolittle, do you know his room number? It was only when he wouldn't leave a message or his name that I decided it was odd."

"Like someone trying to see if she was really a guest here?"

"I guess. I mean, how difficult can it be these days to

connect with a business client? Everyone has cell phones, text messaging, voice mail. Why couldn't he connect without coming to the Paradise on the off chance he would catch up with her?"

"I agree. What did he look like?"

"Hispanic. No accent though so I'm guessing he's a U.S. citizen or has lived here since he was a kid. My thought at the time was that he could be Cuban. Well dressed, linen slacks, nice shirt. He smelled of cigars."

Ginger inhaled sharply. "That's it! That was the scent when I opened Liberty's door. It was a cigar, slightly sweet but very distinctive." She moved to Trout's side. "He was in that room with Liberty."

"We don't know that. Besides, how could he have gotten out? The room was locked."

"Through the Macaw Suite. He could have gone out the window, along the gallery to the Talents' room, down the stairs and out the front door with no one the wiser. It was late, no one on the desk. It could have happened that way." Ginger nodded a self-satisfied nod, "They're in it together."

"It makes a certain kind of sense. There's only one problem. What do they want that they thought would be in Liberty's room?" Trout ran his hand through his hair and tugged at it, as if that would stimulate his brain and give him an answer. "Besides that, he asked for Annette. Why the interest in Liberty's room if he's looking for Annette?"

"There's a connection between the two women," Ginger said. "We need to find out what it is."

"Whatever it is," Trout said, "it got Liberty killed."

"Do you really think so?"

"Yes, I do."

"What about the date rape thing?"

"A cover for the real goal."

"What's that?"

"I have no idea, but I'll bet Annette does."

Chapter Ten

*G*o out to play with the other cats? Really? Is that what Ginger thinks of me, that I'm no more than a kitten, looking for a ball of twine or ... or ... Really! I get no respect. I see no hope for her. After all the trouble I went to in showing her the Talents are up to their eyeballs in this mess, she still thinks of me as a brainless nitwit.

Speaking of which, here are Megs and Bartholomew in the shade of the tiki bar. My hope that they could be useful in this investigation has long since been trashed. Between the two of them they couldn't manage a straight answer if their lives depended on it. Inbreeding aside, I had expected more. They are, after all, cats.

"Still looking for the killer?" *Bartholomew asks, then yawns hugely. He looks as if he will topple over at any moment into a dead sleep.*

"Been up all night?" *I ask in reply.*

"As have you."

"How would you know that?" *I ask.*

"Oh, we get around, don't we Megs?"

Megs stops trying to follow the flight of a butterfly and looks at me. At least, I think she's looking at me. "Busy night," *she says.* "Busy, busy night."

"Doing what?" *I inquire.*

"Watching," *she replies.*

"Anyone or thing in particular?"

"The other spy."

Good grief! These two are impossible.

Bartholomew falls over and begins to snore.

"There were other cats here recently. Have you seen them?" *I ask.*

Megs' eyes open wide. "Other cats? What are they doing here?"

"Not much apparently. I was curious if they were also Hemingway cats."

"I don't know."

"Maybe if I told you their names you might."

"Oh. Well, maybe."

"Lou Costello and Mitzi Gaynor."

Bartholomew snorts in his sleep.

"That's me and Bartholomew," *Megs says.* "Our daily names."

I stare at her, not certain she understood what I told her. "Daily names?"

"Yes. The names people call us. Not our particular names."

"You have more than one name?"

"Three, actually. Don't you?"

Bartholomew coughs and wheezes as he opens his eyes and rights himself. "Are you totally illiterate?"

I'm stunned by his accusation. I'm a cat of superior intelligence, a cat with the power of deduction far greater than that of men. Yet, when I'm in the presence of Megs and Bartholomew, I feel as if I've fallen down the rabbit hole.

"Why do you have three names?"

"Why don't you?" *Bartholomew coughs again.* "Do you at least have a singular name?"

"A singular … I suppose I do. My name is Callahan."

Bartholomew and Megs exchange a look then he lies back down. "Where did you say Warm Springs was?"

"In Georgia."

'Strange customs they have in Georgia." *He yawns and closes his eyes.*

Definitely the rabbit hole. "Okay, Megs, what's your third name?"

"Oh, you never tell your singular name. Never, never, never."

"Why not?"

"It's written that the singular name is one you never confess, it's the name that you know yourself to be, a name no one can ever guess."

"Who wrote such a nonsensical thing?"

"It's a classic, my good man," *says Bartholomew without bothering to open his eyes.* "You should come by the museum and enlighten yourself with some worthwhile literature. Start with T.S. Eliot and go from there. I have grave doubts about Warm Springs."

I can't believe I'm wasting my time on this nonsense. It's time to get back to the business at hand.

"Look," *I say,* "the murderer has been lurking around the Paradise. I caught his scent last night and followed him.

While I was on his trail, someone broke into the bed and breakfast and burgled one of the rooms."

Megs nods. "Yes. The other spy."

"The burglar is also a spy?"

Megs blinks at me as if I have two heads. "No, silly, he burgled the room of the other spy."

"Annette Benoit is a spy?"

"Yes," *Megs says, her voice dropping to a conspiratorial whisper.*

I had a busy night last night and not much sleep. Talking with Megs and Bartholomew doesn't help. In fact, it leaves me with a sense of confusion, a state I definitely don't enjoy. It's times like these that I miss the quiet comforts and common sense of Warm Springs. I bet Lil the Librarian would know what this crazy business of names is all about. Or maybe it's just Key West that's out of tilt, as she would say. I need to find a cozy spot and rest if I'm going to be mentally sharp and get to the bottom of this business of spies, burglars, and murderers. I think I'll try the swing on the front porch of the Paradise. There's always a nice breeze there.

* * *

Ginger hung up the phone. "Duncan says he'll put out a BOLO for the Talents. The information they gave him is the same we have."

"They're long gone by now." Trout said.

"Maybe. If they got what they were after, you're probably right."

The door of the Paradise opened and Sawyer Daniels walked into the foyer. "Hey, Ginger. Trout. What's up?"

"Helping Ginger out. She's short-handed right now."

"Yeah. Heard about the dead woman, Ginger. I guess the law sorted it all out?"

"They're working on it," she said.

"Got any coffee?" Sawyer hitched his shorts up a notch on his belly.

"Sure. Come into the kitchen." She glanced at Trout. "How about you? Want another cup?"

"No thanks," he said, but trailed along behind Ginger and Sawyer. "What brings you to the Paradise, Sawyer?"

"Annette Benoit."

"Oh?" Trout and Ginger said in unison.

Sawyer laughed. "Yes. We have a business meeting in about fifteen minutes."

"What sort of business?" Ginger asked.

Some of the humor left Sawyer's face but he shrugged good naturedly and said, "She has something to sell that I want to buy. At least she thinks I want to buy it."

Sawyer lived in a small apartment down near the marina and he dressed like a down-and-out bum, complete with several days' growth of whiskers. But Ginger and most of the conchs on Key West knew he was in fact a very wealthy man. He bought things on a whim, like the classic sailboat he had Trout refinishing. The money earned by the marina probably didn't cover the costs of maintaining it. Sawyer's money was old family money, the kind that seemed to grow without any effort on Sawyer's part. She was dying to ask him what Annette could possibly have to sell that would interest him, but checked herself.

She poured coffee and cut him a slice of banana nut bread. "Here you go. Sorry to sound so nosey but weird things have been going on around here and I was surprised when you said you had business with Annette. She's French."

Sawyer gave a belly laugh. "What's that got to do with anything?"

Ginger smiled. "I know, I know. It's just that she's

foreign, I guess."

"She's supposed to be in possession of a lost treasure. Very mysterious about it."

"Like Mel Fisher's *Atocha* treasure?" Trout asked.

"I don't know. She said she knew I was a collector and that she had something that was thought to be lost forever, something she knew would be of interest to me."

"So, you agreed to meet with her, just like that?" "Why not? She came to me. All I had to do was walk a few blocks for the sales pitch." He took a bite of the banana nut bread.

"That's funny," Trout said. "You're the second guy looking for Annette this morning. He said he had an appointment with her too."

"She must be trying for a bidding war." Sawyer said. "Who was the other guy, if you don't mind telling me."

"I don't know. Hispanic, maybe Cuban. He wouldn't leave his name."

"Ummm," Sawyer said as he ate another bite of the bread, "you're a fine cook, Ginger."

Ginger wanted to ask more questions but controlled the impulse. Annette had been waiting for a phone call for days. It would appear the expected call was from either Sawyer or the nameless Hispanic. Mystery solved. Sort of.

"You want me to ring her room and let her know you're here?" Ginger asked.

"I don't think she's in," Trout said. "I called her room for the other guy and she didn't answer even though her key isn't on the board."

"She could have been in the shower," Ginger said, but the sudden change in Trout's expression and the pounding of her heart said it could be another reason entirely.

* * *

Trout and Ginger raced from the kitchen and stared at the key board behind the registration desk. Annette's key wasn't there.

"How stupid could I be?" Ginger wailed. "I should have secured the keys after what happened to Liberty. What was I thinking?"

"Don't jump to conclusions. Get the master key. Let's see if she's in her room."

They hurried up the stairs. Ginger took a deep breath and knocked on the door of the Bird Cage. No answer. She knocked again and said, "Ms. Benoit, it's Ginger Browne. I'm coming in."

She placed the key in the lock then looked up at Trout. "It's unlocked."

The door swung open on silent hinges. The room was empty. Someone had slept in the bed at some point after it had been made up the previous morning. A dress lay across the easy chair and a pair of high-heeled sandals looked as if they'd been kicked off and left where they fell. Two of the towels had been used.

"Where's the fire?" Sawyer said from the open doorway.

Ginger jumped when he spoke and pressed a hand to her chest. "Uh, it looks … it looks like she's gone out."

Sawyer looked at his watch. "Maybe she's on her way back. There's still a couple of minutes before we were supposed to meet."

"Right." Ginger swept her hair back from her forehead. Her hand was trembling. "Right. We should lock up the room and go back downstairs."

When she passed through the door, Sawyer said,

"What's going on, Ginger? You look pale as a ghost."

"It's a long story."

"I like long stories."

"It's not for the local gossip mill."

"My lips are sealed."

She studied him a moment. "Come downstairs. I need a drink."

"Now you're talking," he said.

Trout took the keys from Ginger and locked the door of the Bird Cage. "When did you make your appointment with Ms. Benoit?"

"Yesterday afternoon. She called and said she was having a little difficulty making contact with a local authority on the treasure. It wasn't anything to be worried about, she assured me, because she had already been to Boston and spoken with an authenticator there."

"Where   in   Boston?"
"She didn't say. It was all hush-hush. I debated even meeting with her because, to tell the truth, it all sounded like a scam of some kind."

"Why Boston? What kind of treasure could be authenticated there?" Trout frowned. "She gave you no hint of what it might be?"

Sawyer followed Ginger down the stairs. "None."

"It clearly isn't in her room or she wouldn't have left it unlocked." Trout said as he followed Ginger and Sawyer back to the kitchen.

Ginger opened the pantry and took out a bottle of tequila. She poured three shots, cut a lime, and passed them around. Everyone threw back their shots and bit into the lime wedges.

"Better than coffee any day," Sawyer said. "Now tell

me why everyone's so jumpy."

"It started with the dead body."

"That's always a good place to start."

Ginger grinned, her lips began to tremble, then she started giggling. Tears rolled down her cheeks. Trout realized she was on the point of a real meltdown.

"Maybe we should save the tall tales for another day, Sawyer." He went around the table and took Ginger in his arms and made shushing sounds. He sent Sawyer a look and the older man nodded and left the room.

Trout held her for a long time, gently swaying in a soothing motion until she became calm and lifted her head from his chest.

"I'm sorry," she sniffed. "I don't know where that came from."

"Over stressed, a sudden fright. It happens to the best of us."

"Not to me."

"Well, this time it did and that's okay. You're among friends."

She pulled free of his embrace, snatched a paper towel from the holder, and blew her nose. "God, I'm a mess."

"A little focus will help that. You have to let go of the things you can't control, and deal with the rest the best you can. Right now, we need to create a new system for guests coming and going."

"Since I don't appear to have any guests at the moment, it's the perfect opportunity," Ginger said and tried to smile.

"Agreed. Go take all the keys from the board and lock them in the registration desk drawer. The master keys as well. Keep the desk drawer key on a bungee cord on your wrist. You can pass it off to whoever's on duty. That way it's always under your control or that of one of your employees."

"Aye, aye, Captain."

"First problem solved."

"And the next problem?" she asked.

"Call the bartender, what's his name? Harry?

Ginger nodded.

"See if he can fill in for Jules for a few days. Until the convention guests arrive there won't be much demand on the bar and from what I can tell, he spends most of his time reading in the shade."

"He's a student, but yeah, there's little for him to do other than keep the common areas tidy. But I have to have someone out there from tea time forward. People on vacation don't want to have to track down someone to get them a drink when they're idling by the pool."

"Maybe Jules will be back by the time things get really busy. Or Gabriella can give you a few more hours. It doesn't hurt to ask when you need help, Ginger."

"I know, I know, but it's hard for me. I've been trying to manage with as little help as possible. I need to clear enough profit to finish the garage apartment and though Dax isn't expensive, I'm hoping to stretch my resources to cover a sprucing up of the two cottages as well. That would give me extra rental income. The plan for the garage apartment is to have a longer-term tenant, someone living here, maybe working in the tourist trade."

"That's a good plan but right now we need to get through the coming week. Do what you gotta do."

"You're right. I guess I needed someone to tell me what I already knew."

"Good. All of this will get cleared up sooner or later.

Sooner would be nice, but for now, the best way to cope is to focus on the here and now."

"You were good at your job."

Trout squeezed her hand. "It's the same advice anyone would give you. Now let's go see if Annette showed up for her meeting with Sawyer. One less missing guest would be a nice turn of events right now."

* * *

The morning sun has reached my cozy little nesting place on the porch swing. I open my eyes, yawn, and stretch. There's nothing like a power nap when you've been on the job all night. It's still quiet on the streets of Key West. Here in the land of perpetual holiday no one stirs much before mid-morning except fishermen and joggers. What's up with that, anyway? The things humans will expend energy on. Besides, a little extra padding is a good thing, as Trudy the Tour Guide would say.

By the sun's shadow, I see that it's nearing ten o'clock. Time for even the most hungover tourist to be awake and stirring, even on a Sunday. I can't understand the appeal of total intoxication, but it seems to be a favorite pastime of many venturing to the southernmost tip of America, especially the young. I, for one, will guard my little gray cells from such a death but I confess that in my youth I was prone to hit the catnip pretty hard. That and a little bread pudding with whiskey sauce can still tempt me.

Thoughts of food send me in search of Ginger. It has been over two hours since the scone with jam. Delicious though it was, it's hardly enough to fuel a working cat. And I am, once again, refreshed and on the job.

Trout is sleeping on the sofa in the sitting room. It's a well-deserved rest. I find he has proven himself by stepping into the trenches in Ginger's time of need. Well done, Trout. Ginger is polishing the registration desk. All the keys are gone from the board that usually houses them. Her fierce dusting and fluffing and rearranging suggests an almost manic need to regain control of her world. I sympathize with her situation. There's nothing more worrisome than an unsolved murder on your doorstep. Or, in this case, the Toucan Suite.

I hate to interrupt Ginger in her attack on the dust motes that dare reside at the Paradise, so I think I'll check out the premises, see that all is in order. The door of the Macaw Suite is closed. More's the pity. I would dearly love to get my paws on any evidence the Talents left behind. I'm in luck with the Bird Cage. Angela is changing the bed linens. There's a nice view of the pool from here. A light-filled room perfect for an escape from the hustle and bustle of the working world. I don't see why Liberty didn't like it.

Annette isn't a very tidy guest. She has shoes under the bed along with a bit of lacy undergarment. Her clothes are haphazardly hung in the armoire. Tsk tsk, she's even left an uncapped fountain pen here on the window seat and I'm afraid it has ruined the cushion. Ginger won't be pleased. And a sheet of old paper covered by scribbling and scratch outs is caught under the cushion. Annette has very poor penmanship. Maybe this is supposed to be French. Hmmm. Gibberish. And what is this bee in Ginger's bonnet about the French? I'll bet there's an interesting story there. A nice bit of gossip. I confess, I do love a good jaw wag about the comings and goings of humans. Quite often, they are the source of clues hidden in plain sight.

I had hoped for a clue as to why Annette came to Key West in the doldrums of summer but apparently, she has shrugged off the chore that brought her here and is simply enjoying herself. This is the second time that she has stayed out all night. With whom, I wonder?

Ah, well, there's nothing to be learned here. After my nap, I begin to see there might be something to Megs' claims of Annette being a spy. Perhaps not a spy, in the normal sense of the word, but up to something. It's amazing what a little sleep will do for a sharp mind. I should find Megs and see if I can extract more pearls of wisdom from her babble. I'm sure she and Bartholomew can't be far.

* * *

Trout woke with a start. He hadn't intended to fall asleep but rather to be on the look-out for Annette or the Talents. He could see Ginger watering the ferns on the porch. With a yawn, he sat up and realized that he had been in the same clothes for going on three days. A shower and a shave were long overdue.

He went onto the porch and took the watering can from Ginger, refilling it at the spigot at the end of the porch. "No sign of anyone, I take it?"

"No. I changed out the key system like you suggested so anyone returning is going to have to track me down to get into their rooms."

"How about Harry? Did you contact him?"

"He'll be along in about thirty minutes, although I don't see why I'll need him until Wednesday."

"Annette might still return. She didn't make it back until almost two yesterday afternoon. I think she might have found something interesting to occupy her time."

"Maybe. She seemed so concerned about making her business contacts that it's hard for me to believe she wouldn't make the effort to be here for her meeting with Sawyer."

"You have a point," Trout said. He raised the can, heavy with water, up to the hanging ferns. "You might not need Harry after today but I'm glad he's coming. I need to get back to the *Baby Buddha* and clean up a bit. You know what they say about fish and house guests, after three days, throw them out."

"Sorry, Trout. You've been a big help, and it isn't fair of me to impose on you like this."

"Think nothing of it. I didn't have anything else to do."

"Don't worry about me. I'll manage from here." Ginger took the watering can. "I've seen the light and will call in the help I need."

"I'll be back tonight."

"Really, Trout…"

"Dinner would be nice. My cupboard is pretty bare."

Ginger hesitated. "Okay. But after I feed you and the cat, you're going home to get some real rest."

"See you about seven," he said and walked down the steps and away from the Paradise.

The streets were quiet as Trout made his way toward the marina. He stopped in at Sawyer's apartment and knocked. There was no answer. It had occurred to Trout after Sawyer left the Paradise that it was odd Annette would come all the way to Key West to meet with someone that she hadn't made some kind of connection with, before such a costly venture. He tried to remember Sawyer's exact words when asked about their meeting. *She came to me*, he had said.

What difference did it make? Trout asked himself. The real mystery was who killed Liberty and why. Annette's little business venture or scam was beside the point. Or was it? Sawyer was a grown man. A pretty savvy one, too. He could take care of himself. Then why did someone break into Annette's room? There had to be a connection with Liberty, there just had to be. It was too much of a coincidence otherwise.

Trout climbed aboard the *Baby Buddha*, a shower

foremost in his mind. He ducked into the cabin. It took a couple of seconds for his eyes to adjust to the dim light but immediately he knew he was in trouble. Someone had broken into his storage locker and pretty much trashed the boat. All the kitchen cabinets were hanging open. The door to the cubby was ajar and the bedding was on the floor. "Shit!"

He began to sort through his possessions. Whoever it was hadn't done as much damage as he first thought. Nothing was broken, just turned upside down in a very thorough search. When he found his wallet with nine one-hundred-dollar bills still in it, he knew they were after something else. The problem was Trout didn't own anything else of value. Three break-ins, or possibly four, if someone really was in Liberty's room when she arrived home after her night of partying. Someone was desperate to find whatever they were looking for, even to the point of trashing Trout's boat.

* * *

Ginger looked up from the computer at the registration desk to see a very large man in a white linen suit climbing the front steps of the Paradise. He stopped when he gained the front porch and wiped his brow with a handkerchief. By the time he opened the door into the foyer, he was quite flushed. He brought with him the distinct scent of cigars.

"May I help you?" Ginger asked.

"Good afternoon," the man said. "I've been told by one of the local bartenders that the Paradise Bed and Breakfast has the best key lime pie in Key West. Is that true?"

Jerry's handiwork, Ginger thought, and perhaps

Liberty's mysterious man from the Green Parrot. And, perhaps her late-night visitor. "Just about every establishment in the city lays claim to that distinction but I confess I think mine is the best."

"Well, then," he said, "I have come to try it. Do you make it yourself?"

"I do," Ginger smiled, "from my grandmother's recipe."

"Excellent," he said. "A tried-and-true family recipe is generally known to be superior to all these so-called delicacies that are mass produced in some cold sterile pie factory." He wiped his forehead again. "Is it too early to have a sample, with perhaps a cup of Earl Grey tea?"

"Not at all. The Paradise serves tea from three until five-thirty. Your timing is perfect." Ginger came from behind the registration counter. "If you'll follow me."

She seated him in the bay window of the dining room and brought him iced water. The poor man looked like he could use it. "How do you like your tea? Milk or lemon?"

"Milk, please. I've tried to like it with lemon but find my taste can't adapt, kind of like drinking gin and tonic in the winter."

"Around here gin and tonic in the winter isn't very different from the summer."

He laughed. "I see what you mean."

She brought him a pot of tea, properly steeped with boiling hot water, and a piece of her pie artfully embellished with a razor thin slice of lime.

"Are you the proprietress of this lovely establishment?" he asked.

"I am," she replied.

"It's rather a grand old house, isn't it?"

She realized he wanted someone to visit with. Many older people on their own quite often did. Was that why he had sat and talked with Liberty, she wondered. "Yes," she said. "It was built in 1900. My grandmother inherited it from her second husband, and it's been in the family since."

"I can tell it has been lovingly preserved. As we get older, I think we have an affinity with old things, don't you?"

"Perhaps."

"Ah, you're too young to have such nostalgic feelings, but you will one day."

"I'm pretty attached to the old place. It's the only home I've ever known, and it has many memories of my grandmother and mother." She hesitated then said, "I couldn't help but notice that you're a cigar smoker."

"One of my vices, I confess. I've run across a merchant on Wall Street who has some lovely handmade Arturo Fuente cigars. I apologize if my passion for them is offensive."

"No, not at all." Ginger poured him more tea. "I rather like the slightly sweet fragrance."

"You're very tolerant, dear child." He added milk to his tea and took a sip. "The perfect accompaniment to your pie. The bartender was correct, you know. This is the best key lime pie I've tasted, here or anywhere. I daresay the recipe is a highly guarded secret."

"Which bartender told you about the Paradise? I'd like to thank him."

"I don't know his name. He probably told me but, alas, I'm not always good about remembering. Except for pretty young women, of course. Every waiter these days introduces themselves and all those names quickly disappear like mist in the morning sun. But I remember he works at the Green Parrot."

"Probably Jerry."

"You know," he said, "I do believe that was his name. Had a British accent."

"Australian, actually. Would you like another piece of pie?"

"Thank you, no. The world is full of temptations, so I try to savor them in small samples, lest there be no room for others that will surely follow."

"A man of restraint."

He chuckled. "You wouldn't know it by the look of me, but I do try to contain my passions. There's always the unexpected treasure just behind the next door, so to speak."

"If I might be so forward as to ask, do you know a woman named Liberty Anderson?"

He looked at Ginger, cut his eyes upward as if trying to recall, then shook his head. "I don't think so. Where would I know her from, do you think?"

"The Green Parrot, maybe."

"Well, that could be. I've spent some time there in recent days. It's a lively place filled with young people. I like to be surrounded by all that energy and gaiety. One of the pleasures of being my age and having such a, ummm, robust figure, is that they are quite willing to indulge in conversation with me, harmless old man that I am. What does she look like?"

"Blonde…"

"I'm partial to blondes. After redheads, of course."

Ginger smiled. "Life of the party," she continued, "red

dress, very Marilyn Monroe."

"Oh, my, yes. Lovely girl. A bit tipsy but full of life." He frowned. "But I don't think her name was Liberty. That's a name that one would remember. It seems she called herself Stella. Maybe I have the wrong young woman, after all."

"Huh," Ginger gave a little shrug, "could be."

Chapter Eleven

The lizard has become rather bold. He doesn't even flinch when I pass by. Life in paradise seems to have dimmed his reptilian defenses. The island life has worked its magic on him much as it did poor Liberty Anderson. But, regardless of the fact that evil exists even in this bohemian setting, he's safe from me. I haven't the time or inclination to toy with him.

I've seen no sign of Megs and Bartholomew. It would be nice to know who Megs thinks Annette is spying on, unless she has it all wrong and it's the other way around. Perhaps it's time I checked in on Mr. Fortesque. His agents, Ray and Crissy Talent, haven't returned to the Paradise since our encounter at Mallory Pier. I'm afraid my cover is blown, and they know we are on to them. It would never occur to most people that a cat wandering around the city could be a threat to their dark deeds. I'm not so sure about Fat Man, however. He took particular note of my presence when they spied me tailing him. I'll have to be more careful.

People are still having breakfast on the porch of the Curry Mansion Inn. A lazy Sunday brunch is one of their calling cards, I believe. The aroma of several tempting dishes makes my mouth water, but I must stay focused.

Fortesque, from necessity, I imagine, has a room on the ground floor. It doesn't open directly onto the swimming pool, but close enough that my presence won't seem amiss to anyone who might notice. And what is this? His door is open. The maid's cart stands on the pathway outside but there's no sign of her. Am I a lucky cat, or what? Dirty Harry wouldn't consider it luck. He didn't need luck to catch the perp. Is Fat Man the perp? At the very least, I think he's the man behind the curtain. The Wizard of Oz pulling the levers.

The bed is stripped so I know the maid will return soon. I must be quick, in and out, in the time I have. This worn leather attaché seems promising. Worn, perhaps, but very expensive leather. A small, highly polished rectangle of brass is attached near the lock. There is writing on it. A brand? A name? Who knows. But, again, lucky me. Just a nudge of the paw, and, oh my, it tips over, spilling some of the contents. Documents, documents, stationery, postage stamps. The man has a veritable office with him. Let's see if anything here gives a hint of why he has come to Key West.

* * *

Trout ran a hand across his jaw and examined his face in the small rectangle of mirror in the tiny head of the *Baby Buddha*. Close enough, he decided. After a couple of hours sleep, he was feeling himself again. The boat had been restored to order, his wallet now securely in his back pocket. He had donned his best old Hawaiian print shirt and his only pair of long pants. He wasn't sure why. It was just dinner with Ginger at the Paradise. *Right.*

He stopped by Sawyer's apartment when he left the pier. Still no one home. On a hunch, he decided to check in at the marina office. Mikey was there trying to fix a Penn Fierce II reel. It kept catching.

"Thought those were supposed to hold up under any kind of misuse."

"Aye. They're supposed to."

Mikey wasn't in the best humor.

"Did you see anyone around the marina earlier?"

"Lots of people."

"Anyone who didn't look like they belonged?"

"How's that look?"

"Never mind," Trout said. "Do you know anyone who might be interested in taking on one of my charters?"

"Depends. When is this charter?" Mikey asked.

"Wednesday morning. Six o'clock."

Mikey looked out through the windows of the marina office, along the long pier of docked boats. "Maybe J.J. He's got a new baby. Could probably use the extra cash." He glanced up at Trout. "Why? I thought you were broke."

"Taking a personal day," Trout said.

Mikey stared at him a long heartbeat, then returned his attention to the fishing reel.

"Know where I might find Sawyer?"

"Gone."

"Gone? Where?"

Mikey shrugged. "Don't know. Drove him into Miami about eleven."

"Where in Miami?"

Mikey looked up from the task in hand. "Why?"

"Curious," Trout said.

"Curiosity killed the cat."

"So they say."

"Uh, huh."

"I don't suppose you dropped him at the airport?"

"Can't say."

"Right." Trout stood, watching Mikey fish pull line from the reel. "Will he be back anytime soon?"

"What's the emergency?"

"Nothing. He missed an appointment with a woman at the Paradise. I'm headed that way. Seemed important, but maybe not."

"Maybe not."

It was obvious Mikey wasn't going to tell Sawyer's business. That was one reason Sawyer kept him around, Trout supposed. A good gofer is one who can keep your secrets.

Trout stepped out of the marina office and stood a moment, enjoying the sun lowering in the western sky. The days were already getting shorter, little by little, but here in the land of forever summer, the seasons didn't change much except for the hours of sunlight. He dreaded the coming of long winter nights. In the light of day, it was so much easier to keep the shadows at bay.

He turned from the view and let his thoughts wander to Ginger of the Titian red hair. He had a decision to make. Perhaps it had already been made. Events seemed to be conspiring to throw them together. What he knew he had to do now was decide whether or not he would keep resisting. Or if he was still capable of doing so.

It was a peaceful walk along Duval Street at this hour of the day. The only real activity was a couple in front of the Gold Empire convenience store checking their scratch-offs to see if they were lottery winners. Trout was about to cross the street when the door of the Starbucks opened and Mel Anderson stepped out, a tall coffee in hand.

"Mrs. Anderson," he said.

She gave a start and looked up at him. "Mr...."

"Trout," he said.

"From the Paradise."

"I thought you'd be on your way back to D.C. by now."

"So would I, but apparently nothing happens in this sauna of a hell-hole on the weekend."

"What seems to be the problem?"

"Arty. They won't let me have him."

"Why?"

"Bureaucracy. What else?"

"Well, maybe they'll be able to sort things out to-morrow."

"You've obviously never worked for the government."

Trout made no comment.

"Monday's the day everyone spends getting over the weekend. Nothing gets done."

"Speaking from experience, are you?" Trout suppressed the urge to laugh.

It was Mel's turn to be uncommunicative.

"Things might be different this time," Trout said.

"Hello?" she said. "Do you even know where you are?" Trout grinned. Mel was probably right.

"This place is costing me a fortune. If that hussy wasn't already dead, I'd kill her."

"Huh. Well, good luck with the authorities."

Mel nodded and set off in the direction from which he had come.

Duncan would have been smart to give her the ashes, Trout thought as he continued along Duval Street.

He was greeted by the smell of red meat searing on hot metal when he rounded the corner of the bed and breakfast and crossed the lawn to an outdoor kitchen near the back entrance into the Paradise.

"This is a rare treat," he said, as Ginger looked up from the grill.

She smiled. "I decided we could both use a little boost of iron."

"Can I help?"

"Open the wine so it can breathe. Everything else is ready."

"You shouldn't have gone to so much effort."

"It's all easy enough; steak, salad, fruit. How do you like your steak?"

"Medium rare." He said as he opened the wine.

"Good choice." She turned the meat and offered up her glass.

Trout poured for both of them. "How'd your afternoon go?"

"Interesting," she said, then told him about the visit from the man from the Green Parrot.

"You think it's the same guy?"

"It'd be hard to imagine two men fitting that description being in Key West at the same time."

"Agreed." Trout savored the red wine. Ginger knew her stuff. The steaks were resting under aluminum foil while she tossed the salad.

"Do you believe him about coming to the Paradise for pie?"

"It would be a strange coincidence even though Jerry

has been talking things up for me."

"And you don't believe in coincidences."

"Exactly."

"What do you think he wanted?"

"I'm as puzzled as you are. The conversation was nothing but small talk. He freely admitted seeing Liberty or someone who fit her description. He did talk about life's pleasures and his vices. Nothing specific other than cigars and pie but there was a sense of expectation, as if he was waiting for something."

"Did you think he was fishing for information?"

"Not that I could tell."

"Odd."

"Very." She plated the salad. "How was your afternoon? Get any sleep?"

"You could say it was equally eventful."

"How so?"

"Someone broke into the *Baby Buddha* and trashed the place."

"Oh, Trout! No!" Ginger's hand went to her throat. She had a stricken look on her face.

"No real damage but a very thorough search."

"What did they take?"

"Nothing that I could tell." He felt reassuringly of his back pocket. "They left behind a lot of expensive fishing gear and my pocket change."

"What were they after?"

"Good question."

"Do you think it was simply for the sake of mischief? An act of vandalism?"

"No."

"It has to be connected to what's going on here." Ginger's forehead was drawn into lines of concern.

"That's what I'm thinking."

She placed the salad plates on the small bistro table by the pool. It was laid with fresh white linens and held a small bouquet of daisies. Trout refilled their wine glasses and placed them on the table.

They moved the conversation to other things while they enjoyed their meal—the renovation of the garage apartment, the dread of Fantasy Fest and all the madness and debauchery it would bring at the end of October. The event was a double-edged sword. The Paradise was always full, but the clientele tended to be out of control for a span of ten days. Ginger and all her staff would be run off their feet.

The steak Ginger served Trout was enough meat for a man twice his size, but he made good headway with it. When he sat back in his chair and drained the last of the wine in his glass, he said, "You're one hell of a good cook, Ginger."

"Anyone can throw a piece of meat on a fire."

"Take the compliment, it's well deserved. It isn't just the steak, or the right wine, it's all the little details, all the time and energy you spend on everything to make your business a success. You should be proud of all you've accomplished."

Ginger blushed and looked away from his steady gaze. "I'm always comparing myself to my mother. Or my grandmother. For them, everything was always effortless and everyone who came to the Paradise had the most wonderful experiences. Many of them came back year after year." She shrugged. "Mom and Gran had an ease about them, you know? People felt like family or old comfortable friends."

"I feel that way. I'm sure your guests do, too."

Trout could see that the personal nature of the conversation was making Ginger uncomfortable. She said, "Speaking of guests, there's been no sign of Annette or Ray and Crissy Talent. I called Duncan to see if he wanted to fingerprint their room before I cleaned it, but he already had a set from the initial break-in. They're not in any criminal data base so there's that at least. I'm leaving everyone's things in place tonight, but tomorrow I'm packing it all up." She shifted in her chair. "I'm beginning to worry about Annette."

"Me too."

"Duncan said he'd have the patrols keep an eye out for her. She's not officially missing yet. It's been less than twenty-four hours. He's going to run her passport and see if he can learn anything helpful."

"It occurred to me that neither of us saw her leave last night. She came back to the Paradise because she broke the heel on her shoe. That was early evening. I went to the hospital with Jules, and you dealt with the police and locked up. We assumed she was in her room all that time because her key wasn't on the board."

"I've worried with that all afternoon. She could easily have left while I cleaned the coffee spill and print powder from the pantry. For some reason, I just assumed she wouldn't go out after the fright she had."

"Maybe the incident spooked her, especially after what happened to Liberty."

"But where would she go?" Ginger asked.

"I don't know. Another hotel, maybe."

"Possibly, but she left all her things."

"No one is behaving as they should," Trout said with a sigh.

* * *

Ginger looked around at the rustling coming from the cast iron plants. Callahan strolled from the foliage and came to inquire about his dinner. She smiled. "Where are your sidekicks?" she asked.

The cat looked up at her with an expression that she could have sworn said, *Oh, please.*

"Do you ever get the impression he knows what we're saying?" she asked Trout.

"Actually, I get the feeling he thinks we haven't a clue about anything."

"Well," she said, "he is a cat."

"Meaning?"

"They know they're superior and love toying with us."

"If you say so."

"Ever read *Old Possum's Book of Practical Cats*?"

The cat's ears twitched.

"Nope. But I saw the play."

"Yeow." Callahan said.

"Well?" Ginger asked.

"I think Eliot had too much time on his hands."

"Men." Ginger said and smiled as she stood to do Callahan's bidding. "I hope you like your steak medium rare, and a bit cold." She took their leftovers to the outdoor kitchen area and cut some of Trout's T-bone into small bits. "I'm saving the rest for Dax," she said to the cat. "He's been working long hours on the apartment and it's beginning to shape up. I wonder where he's gotten off to tonight?"

The cat seemed unconcerned about his companion's welfare. As soon as Ginger placed the scraps of meat on a bread-and-butter plate on the brick pavers beside the grill, he tucked into it with gusto.

Ginger returned to the table and helped Trout gather the remaining dishes and cutlery. They took them into the kitchen and began to wash up.

As Trout dried the wine glasses and returned them to the china cabinet, Ginger went through to the foyer and found Harry reading a textbook. "All quiet?" she asked.

Harry sat back on the high stool behind the registration desk and nodded.

"You might as well go on home. It looks like it's an empty house tonight. No need for you to have a restless night on the daybed."

"You're sure?" Harry asked.

Ginger nodded. "I'll take the key."

Harry took the bungee cord from his wrist and gave it to Ginger. "You need me to come in tomorrow morning? I don't have a class until eleven."

"No," Ginger sighed. "All that needs doing will be cleaning the Bird Cage and the Macaw Suite. I can handle that. Angela has the day off tomorrow as well. But I'll need you back at one on Wednesday. The conventioneers should be arriving by then."

"Cool." Harry collected his book and cell phone and strolled out the front door of the Paradise.

Ginger placed the door on auto lock and dimmed the lights on the front porch. When she entered the kitchen, Trout had stored the leftovers in the refrigerator and wiped down the worktable. He was drying the kitchen sink.

He looked up from this task and said, "What next?"

"Nothing. There's no need to do the breakfast set-up. It would be a waste of food and effort. If Annette shows up before morning, I can handle whatever she might need easy enough." She frowned. "I wonder if Sawyer ever caught up with her."

"I don't think so. He left town right after he was here."

"Where'd he go?"

"Mikey wouldn't say but I'd suspect he went to Boston."

"Because that's where Annette went before coming to Key West. To get authentication."

"I also think Sawyer has an idea of what Annette is hawking. It must be something of serious value for him to take off like that."

"Boston is a maritime city like Key West. Perhaps it has to do with ships and sunken treasure after all."

"We won't know until one of them shows up and spills the beans," Trout said.

"You're right." She looked around the tidy kitchen. "Thanks, Trout. Not just for this but for everything. I know you didn't want to be drawn into this mess."

Trout came around the table and took Ginger's hand. "I'm glad I was here."

"Me too," she said and looked up into his pale blue eyes. "I sent Harry home. There was no need for him to …"

"Ginger," Trout slowly drew her into his arms and kissed her.

* * *

Finally, Trout and Ginger have stopped dancing around the inevitable. The only problem with that is they'll be distracted in a major way. Not that I can't handle this case on my own, but an opposable thumb would come in handy at the moment. I'll leave them to it. I need to figure out how to get into the Bird Cage. This business of spilled beans is enlightening. The king of the conchs is looking to buy something from Annette Benoit. If Megs' ramblings are anything to go by, I'll bet my whiskers that Annette was originally intended to occupy the Toucan Suite. I need to get back into both rooms.

Chapter Twelve

Ginger made a small carafe of coffee and poured a cup. She went to stand at the kitchen window overlooking the back grounds of the Paradise. She watched Dax as he neatly stacked scraps of wood from the renovation of the garage apartment on the side of the structure, then placed a lattice screen around them. Everything was green, lush, and tidy. For the first time in days, she felt at peace. With no guests at the bed and breakfast she could be leisurely.

"Good morning," Trout said from the doorway to the hall.

Ginger turned and smiled. "Morning."

He crossed the room to where she stood. "Smells good," he said, then he took her cup, set it on the window sill, and kissed her.

He was a good kisser. A very good kisser. The nice thing about good kisses, Ginger thought, was that they led to other very nice things. "How'd you sleep?" she asked.

"Seriously?"

She smiled more broadly, and he kissed her again.

"Breakfast?" she asked when he finally broke away.

"Might be a good idea," he said and grinned. "Before I get a better idea."

Ginger felt the blush all over her body. "Probably a good idea," she agreed. "It's a work day, after all."

"You always get up this early?"

"That's the life," she said. "Usually, I'm baking something fresh for my guests by now. In fact, I feel like a sluggard this morning. I don't know when I last had a free morning."

"You should hire more help."

"That's a luxury only the bigger establishments can afford. The house is old, the upkeep high, and people are accustomed to five-star service these days."

"Ever think of doing anything else? Something less demanding?"

"I won't deny it's crossed my mind once or twice. But it's what I know and, as you reminded me last night, I'm good at it. My mother once told me that a man's arms around you always felt good, but a man and his embrace came and went. The Paradise would always be here."

"Sounds like your mother was a wise woman."

"Life does that to you, I guess."

"What about your father? Or were his the arms that came and went?"

"A psychologist, huh?"

"Sorry."

"It's okay. I get my red hair from him. Sailor Sam. My mother always referred to him that way. Not my husband or your father, just Sailor Sam. He was with the naval base when they met and married, but like the tide, he came and went. He was stationed in Guam, Hawaii, California for a while."

"Your mother didn't move with him?"

"No. Gran needed her here and I don't think she really wanted to go. Maybe she realized early on that he couldn't stay, and she couldn't leave."

"What happened to him?"

"I don't know." Ginger went to the coffee pot and refilled her cup. She took down a clean one for Trout and filled it as well. "He used to turn up once in a while when I was little but at some point, he stopped."

"Did they divorce?"

"No. I don't think so. You have to remember my mother and grandmother were conchs. Life down here isn't the same as the mainland. No one worries too much about the formalities. I suppose he could be anywhere. He could be dead."

"You have no desire to find out?"

"No. I never knew him, and between my grandmother and my mother, I never needed him. I suppose I would have turned out differently if I'd had a father, but maybe not."

"What would you have done differently, do you think?"

Ginger shrugged. "Gotten married I suppose. I came close. He was from Iowa."

"Iowa?" Trout grinned. "I can't picture you in Iowa."

Ginger arched an eyebrow and smiled. "Why ever not?"

"Maybe it's the red hair. I don't think it would work anywhere but here, against all this green foliage. And the brown eyes, very tropical."

"Funny man."

"Your mother must have lived a lonely life if he disappeared when you were young."

"I didn't say my mother was alone. Men came into her life and, I guess you could say, her arms. They came and they went but it wasn't a strife-filled coming and going. As I said, she and my grandmother had an ease about them. They embraced the life they had and were content."

"Next you'll be telling me things about your grandmother that would make me blush."

"She was married three times. She buried the first two, my grandfather, then her second husband who left her the Paradise, although at the time it was her home, not a bed and breakfast. The third one wandered off to the mainland and never returned."

"Wow."

Ginger realized she'd said too much. She turned to the bread box, opened it, and busied herself with finding the freshest of the croissants. "Just so you know," she said, her back to Trout.

Trout came to the counter where she worked and took the bread from her hands. He turned her so she faced him. "I was married," he said. "Twice." With that he took her by the hand. "Just so you know." Then he led her out of the kitchen and down the hallway toward the back of the Paradise.

* * *

It was getting late in the morning by the time Trout and Ginger stood in the open doorway to the Bird Cage. No one had touched it since Angela made up the bed the previous morning.

"You're sure about this?" he asked.

"Her reservation ended with the eleven o'clock check-out today. She's been gone nearly forty-eight hours. I don't know what else to do. Besides, I have guests for every room in the place on Wednesday."

"Okay. Where should we start?"

"Well, the bed is fine. There are clean towels in the bathroom. I suppose I just need to pack up her things, dust, and make sure there's nothing in the bathroom."

Trout ducked into the bathroom and brought out a flimsy robe. "It was on the hook on the back of the door."

Ginger took the suitcase from the bottom of the armoire and opened it on the bed. "Everything in here, I guess. I'll keep it in storage." She started gathering the items on the dressing table. One of the pots of cream was open. She lifted it to her nose and inhaled, closing her eyes as she did. "Expensive stuff," she said. Then she screwed the lid on and placed it in the suitcase.

Along with her clothing, shoes, and unmentionables, there was a valise. Ginger was hesitant to look inside but Trout wasn't so squeamish.

"An iPad," he said, "some business cards…"

"What do they say?"

He turned one toward the window for better light. "Annette Benoit, *Representante Literaire*, and a phone number. Foreign, odd sequence, probably French," he said.

"Representative of what? You think that means literature?"

"I don't speak French but that would be my guess."

"Here," she held out her hand and Trout placed the card in it. "I'll call the number when we finish and see what we can learn."

Trout placed the suitcase of Annette's belongings in the hallway and took a feather duster to the top of the highboy and the posts on the bed.

Ginger laughed. "If you could see yourself. All you need is a short black skirt and a white apron and cap."

"One of your favorite fantasies, I suppose?"

"My favorite fantasy is a maid, regardless of black skirt and apron, to do this every day for free."

"While you lounge by the pool eating bonbons and sipping champagne, no doubt. Well, madam, your wish is my command," he said with an awkward curtsey.

Ginger shook her head and turned to the window seat. She snatched up the cushion and swore under her breath.

"What?" Trout asked.

She held up a pretty pillow covered in a tropical print chintz. "Ink all over the cushion. It's ruined." She felt along the wooden structure of the seat and found the uncapped pen. "I really loved this pattern."

"It wasn't a cherished heirloom, was it?"

"No." She sighed. "And I've had worse things happen. I'm still sometimes amazed what total intoxication can make a normal person think is reasonable behavior." She took the pillow to the laundry cart and stacked it on top of the waste bin.

As she turned back into the room, she glimpsed a tiny corner of paper under the bed. She bent down and retrieved it. Also lurking beneath the bed was a pair of sandals and some lacy panties. She made a note to herself to speak to Angela and Gabriella about the meaning of the words *thorough* cleaning. The shoes and undergarment went into the suitcase. After a quick glance at the piece of paper, she added it to the trash.

With one last check of the bathroom, she said, "That does it, I think."

As Ginger locked the room, Trout glanced down the hallway to the emergency escape window. There on the landing were the two Hemingway cats, Lou Costello and Mitzy Gaynor. "I think those two have taken up residence at the Paradise."

Ginger followed the direction of his gaze. "They have been around a lot lately. It's unusual to see them so often but maybe that's because of Callahan. Curiosity killed the cat."

Trout stood there staring. Something about the phrase niggled at the back of his mind. What was it that this image was trying to trigger? The two cats sat there staring back at him.

* * *

I top the stairs to the escape window of the Paradise and find Megs and Bartholomew staring into the building. "I've been looking for you two," *I say.*

"Why?" *Bartholomew asks.*

"I need to know why Megs thinks Annette is a spy, and I need to get into the Bird Cage."

"You just missed your chance," *Megs says.*

I look into the window and catch a glimpse of the maid's cart being pushed around the corner and out of sight of the Bird Cage by Trout. I realize I've dallied too long at the museum checking out

Hemingway's writing studio. The forces surrounding the murder at the Paradise are gathering and I needed to be sure of my facts.

"How did you know Annette was a spy?" *I ask Megs.*

"She hides things."

"What things?"

"Black things."

"With red trim," *Bartholomew adds.*

"How do you know she hides things?"

"We watch," *Megs says.*

"What do these things look like?" *I ask.*

"Not too big," *Bartholomew says.*

"And not too small," *Megs says.*

I want to bash my head against the window. Instead, I ask, "Bigger than a breadbox?"

"What's a breadbox?" *she wants to know.*

I search my memory for something a cat could relate to. "Is it like your bed cushion?"

"I don't know," *Megs replies,* "I haven't slept on it."

This is pointless. I'll have to go with my suspicions and see where that gets me. Megs and Bartholomew aren't going to be any help.

I hear a car door slam and I look toward the street. Fat Man, H. Fortesque, to be more precise, has just emerged from a stretch limousine and is making his way to the front porch of the Paradise. Interesting, most interesting. I hurry down the stairs and in through the back door of the bed and breakfast.

By the time H. Fortesque reaches the foyer of the Paradise, I'm sitting, waiting, anxious to see what brings The Mountain to Mohammed.

Chapter Thirteen

Ginger heard the closing of the front door and came down the stairs to find the connoisseur of key lime pie standing in the foyer mopping his brow with a handkerchief.

"Hello. Again," she said. "Back for more pie?"

He smiled and angled his head a bit in a bashful acknowledgment that she wasn't fooled by his subterfuge. "Ms. Browne," he said in a winded voice. "You'll forgive me while I catch my breath. Exertion is no friend to a fellow of my physique, especially in this climate."

Ginger motioned with her hand toward the sitting room. "Please, come have a seat."

"Thank you." He followed her into the spacious, light-filled room and wisely took the center of a loveseat.

"Can I get you anything? A glass of water?"

"That would be lovely."

As Ginger turned toward the foyer, Trout strolled into the room.

"Hello." He came to a stop a few feet from where the man sat.

"Good afternoon." Fortesque mopped his forehead once again with the handkerchief. "August is not the ideal month to visit Key West, is it?"

"Depends," Trout said, "on why you're here."

He chuckled. "Right to the point. I like that." He offered Trout his hand and as they shook, he said, "Heronimous Fortesque at your service."

"Armentrout Richardson."

Fortesque inclined his head. "Admirable name."

"Likewise."

Ginger appeared on the tail end of this exchange with the glass of water. "What can we do for you, Mr. Fortesque?"

He took a long drink of the water and placed the glass on the side table. "That was refreshing. Thank you." He looked from Ginger to Trout. "I'm here to see Ms. Benoit."

"The literary agent," Ginger said on a hunch.

"Ah. So you know the story."

"Why don't you tell us your version?" Trout asked.

A look of cunning appeared in Fortesque's eyes. "Where is Ms. Benoit?"

"She's not here at the moment," Ginger said. *He knows we're fishing,* she thought. "She missed her other appointment as well," she added in the hope it would appear they knew more about what was going on.

"So, Ray was right," Fortesque said.

"About what?" Trout asked.

"The other bidder."

"Where are Ray and Crissy Talent, Mr. Fortesque?" Ginger asked.

He smiled. "I imagine they're happily counting their good fortune in a little bungalow off Flagler."

"Then they're not from Tennessee after all," she said.

"It was a ruse since a local would hardly be booking a room at the Paradise. In the end it was easier to pay them off than allow them to proceed in their blundering way and risk drawing attention to the negotiations."

"Alerting someone like the other cigar aficionado, you mean?"

For an instant Trout thought he had caught Fortesque off guard. But just as quickly the man regained his composure.

Fortesque openly assessed Trout. After a long pause, he said, "Ah. Has Ms. Benoit met with this other," he waved his hand as if summoning the word he wanted from the air, "collector."

"Is that what you are?" Trout asked. "A collector."

"Didn't Ms. Browne tell you?"

"She said you liked pie."

Fortesque laughed. "Yes, I like pie. I like many things."

"Old things," Ginger said. "Treasures that tempt you, that's your passion, isn't it?"

Fortesque tilted his head slightly in acknowledgement.

"What were Ray and Crissy Talent doing for you, Mr. Fortesque? Are those their real names?"

Fortesque's brows shot up in a look of amusement. "Does it really matter?"

"Detective Moore thinks so. Murder is serious

business," Trout said.

Fortesque tut-tutted Trout and Ginger. "No one could seriously think those two capable of murder. Ineptitude, certainly, but not murder."

"We know they were in Liberty Anderson's room and that she was murdered. Inept or not, that's pretty damning," Trout said.

"They also lured her away from the Chart Room Bar when she was too drunk to resist," Ginger added.

"This is all very melodramatic," Fortesque said. "How can you possibly know it was them? The truth of the matter is that the unfortunate dead woman had nothing to do with me or my associates." He saw the look on Ginger's face. "Yes, yes, I know about the woman who died in one of your rooms. The whole island knows. She has nothing to do with my business here."

"What is your business, Mr. Fortesque?" Trout asked.

Fortesque smiled. "Private. And it will stay that way until I've met with Ms. Benoit. After that, I'll be happy to tell your Detective Moore all about the miscreant Talents. They're harmless bumblers but I'll let him find that out for himself. Now," he said as he gathered himself to rise from the loveseat, "I'll be on my way." When he had regained his balance, he turned to Ginger and said, "Be so kind as to tell Ms. Benoit I called when she returns."

With that he made his way to the foyer and out the door of the Paradise.

* * *

"What do you make of that?" Trout asked Ginger as they watched Fortesque climb into the limousine.

"One of Mr. Fortesque's vices is rare things of great value and importance. Since Ms. Benoit's a literary agent, that suggests a rare old book of some kind, possibly one of Hemingway's books, since a number of people interested in what she has to offer have descended on Key West."

"Like a first edition?"

"Maybe. But all this secrecy suggests something more than that."

"And I know just the man to ask," Trout said. He gave Ginger a solid kiss and left the Paradise.

He hadn't gone two blocks when he realized the cat was following him. Trout thought briefly that Ginger might worry about Callahan straying, then laughed. The cat had a mind and will of his own. What Ginger wanted didn't figure into the equation. Just then he saw Mel Anderson coming out of the First Bank of the Florida Keys and he stopped in his tracks. She was counting money which she then stuffed into her purse.

"Huh," he said to the cat. "Wonder what she's still doing in Key West?" Then he remembered her complaint about the difficulty of getting anything done with government bureaucracy on a Monday and smiled. Crusty old bat probably deserved the aggravation and expense, he decided.

With a shake of his head, he walked on to the marina. Mikey was just coming out of the office when Trout climbed the steps.

"The boss back yet?"

Mikey jerked his head in the direction of the office door and continued on down the steps.

The bell over the door jangled when Trout opened it. Sawyer Daniels looked up from his computer screen at the sound and grinned. "Yo, Trout. Heard you were looking for me."

"How was Boston?" Trout asked.

Sawyer grinned more broadly. "Couldn't really say."

Trout let his gaze travel around the very club-like surroundings of the marina office. A glass case contained an old boat captain's cap. Three shot glasses held pride of place before a photograph of Ernest Hemingway, Joe Russell, and a huge black man. "Who's the big guy?" Trout asked.

"Big Skinner," Sawyer said and leaned his chair back, his hands clasped behind his head. "Bartender at the Blind Pig. That would be Russell's first saloon after the end of Prohibition, before it became Sloppy Joe's and changed locations."

There was a second photograph of Hemingway on a boat, probably the *Pilar*, Trout thought. "I hadn't realized you were such a fan of Hemingway." He looked from the photographs to Sawyer. "I've never seen you crack the spine of a book."

"It's not about the books, it's about the man." Sawyer rose from his chair and came to look at the photographs with Trout. "If I'd been around when they sold the house after his death, I'd have beaten Bernice Dickson to it."

Callahan wended his way between Sawyer's legs. "Got yourself a boat cat, huh?"

"No, he followed me from the Paradise." Trout jangled the change in his pocket. "What did you find out at the JFK Library?"

Sawyer was silent for a minute then shook his head. "You're a nosey cuss, Trout. It's not good to meddle in other people's business."

"Ginger's in trouble. The whole island is talking about the death in the Paradise. The place is empty."

"What happened to the Benoit woman?"

"That's your concern? I thought you said Ginger was good people."

"She is, and nothing bad's going to happen to her or the Paradise except they'll probably add her to the ghost tours route. That's not necessarily a bad thing, you know."

"What's the Benoit woman fencing?"

"Let's call it a silent auction, huh?" Sawyer went to his desk, sat down and leaned back in his chair, eyeing Trout.

Callahan jumped onto the desktop.

"It's all hush, hush," Sawyer said. "Supposedly someone approached her with a lost piece of personal property that belonged to Hemingway, from his days on the continent."

"She's a literary agent. It doesn't take an Einstein to figure out it has something to do with his writing." Trout moved to the desk and scratched the cat's ears. "What did you find out in Boston?"

Sawyer eyed Trout, gave a solitary shake of his head and said, "That it's possible but highly improbable."

"What is it?"

"Don't know for sure."

"But you went looking for confirmation of something specific, so you have to have a pretty good idea."

"I do, Trout, but I'm not sharing. Not right now. After I meet with Ms. Benoit, then we'll see. The truth of the matter is that I'm still leaning heavily toward this being an elaborate scam."

"What do you know about Liberty Anderson? What does she have to do with all this?"

"Nothing. Duncan said it was a date rape thing gone

south. There'll be a manslaughter charge in it at the very least if they can find who did it."

"You haven't had anyone snooping around the Paradise, have you?"

Sawyer's voice was sharp when he answered. "I wouldn't do that to Ginger."

"Do you know Fortesque?"

"The whale? Yeah, I know him. We've crossed paths in the past."

"Is he capable of pushing the envelope as far as murder?"

"I wouldn't think so, but I don't know. Besides, the dead woman has nothing to do with what we've got going on."

"I think she was killed by mistake."

Sawyer sat up straighter in his chair. "You think someone was after Annette Benoit?"

"That's the only thing that fits the facts so far. They're both blonde, rather flamboyant, and they arrived at the Paradise within a day of each other. I think someone got them confused."

"Do you think whoever it was got what they were after?"

"I don't know. Annette is missing. There's been no sign of her for nearly forty-eight hours. Yet Mr. Fortesque is still here and both of you are still eager to find Annette and her highly lucrative artifact. Could someone else be after the same item?"

"There's always that possibility."

"Any idea who the Cuban is?"

Sawyer hesitated. "I couldn't say for sure. There's one possibility. Geraldo Mechoso. His grandfather worked on the Hemingway farm, *Finca Vigia*, in Cuba. Ernesto,

Geraldo's grandfather, would tell stories of him and the children. This was when Hemingway was married to his third wife, Martha. Geraldo supposedly has some correspondence from their friendship. It's rumored that he also has an early draft of *For Whom the Bell Tolls*, but it's just that, a rumor."

"Would he be in the running for this mysterious treasure Annette is trying to sell?"

"I doubt it. He has a cigar factory and does all right but not the kind of money he would need for something like this."

"Whatever *this* is," Trout said.

Sawyer just grinned.

Chapter Fourteen

I *now know the what of this Gordian Knot. A rare lost manuscript has supposedly surfaced. At least, that's what Annette is trying to auction off to a pack of avid collectors. Lil the Librarian was quite fond of Hemingway. She read one of his biographies to me over a damp, cold winter. Sadly, the biographer didn't share Hemingway's sparse writing style. She also read quite a bit of Faulkner that year. Did I mention it was a long winter?*

From what I remember, a lot of Hemingway's writing was kind of autobiographical. Which, I suppose, makes it easy to follow his career. What then could Annette Benoit possibly have that hasn't already been published or documented? Nothing. I think Ms. Benoit is a con-artist.

Be that as it may, if the con is believed, then there might be someone out there who wants what she's offering badly enough to kill her for it. Two victims for different motives in the same place at the same time is too much of a coincidence. That means either they're in cahoots on this caper or one of these women is an unintended victim. Which one is it?

Trout thinks it's Liberty. He's right in that no motive for her death has surfaced except an attempt at date rape; a rape that didn't occur. Could something have scared the rapist off? I have to allow that's a possibility and that Liberty's death is the tragic accidental overdose it appears to be. Then why was Mechoso in her room?

We need to find Geraldo Mechoso. If Sawyer is correct, his connection to Hemingway is a tenuous one at best. But, of one thing I'm sure. The scent of cigars has been the calling card for each intrusion into the Paradise and I can't believe that it's Fat Man.

Could Mechoso have followed Liberty, thinking she was the literary agent? I can see how drugging her would facilitate a search of her room but how did he get in and out? If he accompanied her back to the Paradise, he could have gone up with her, with no one to witness it. But how to leave without the key being on the wrong side of the locked door? If the Talents were in the employ of H. Fortesque, and the center room, the Flamingo Suite, was occupied by the guests who fled the B & B as soon as Liberty's body was discovered, how did Mechoso escape without being seen?

* * *

The morning had been a wonderful interlude in the midst of all that was going on at the Paradise but now Ginger felt unsettled by the visit from Fortesque. On the surface, it appeared that two separate things had happened at the bed and breakfast in a short window of time. Liberty had been poisoned by a person, or persons, unknown for reasons unknown. Duncan thought she was the intended victim of an attempt at date rape. There was no physical evidence that an actual rape had occurred.

The second incident was the arrival of Annette Benoit from France by way of Boston, Massachusetts. What information had she been seeking there? Fortesque had hired the Talents to follow her. Were they responsible for the attempt to break into the Toucan Suite as well? If so, was it as Fortesque said, that they were incompetent? Could this have led them to break into the wrong room? Did one of them actually succeed in gaining access to Annette's room? If not, then who had done those things, sending first her, then Jules, to the hospital?

More and more it seemed to Ginger that the two women had some connection. How to find that connection was the problem.

She needed to let Duncan know the Talents were local. If he could pick them up for questioning, they might get some answers to these questions. Until then, there was no way to know how, or if, Liberty's death was connected to the missing literary agent. But one thing was certain in Ginger's mind. Two such mysterious events couldn't be a coincidence, especially in light of the fact that Annette was missing.

Ginger remembered the business card and dug it out of her back pocket. She started to dial the number with her cell phone, then hesitated. What to say to whoever answered, she wondered. The best approach, she decided, was to act knowledgeable about Annette's business in Key West. Maybe her secretary would let something slip.

After a long, silent few seconds, the number from Annette's business card began to ring. It was a short-lived victory. The second ring activated her voice mail and Ginger received a greeting in French. She supposed it was a request that she leave a message, so she did. Only time would tell if this would get a response.

Worrying about all these loose threads of fact and speculation was giving her a headache. Make a list, she decided, a grocery list of last-minute items for the incoming on Wednesday. She always found that a distraction freed the mind to seek its own answers.

Breakfast wouldn't be necessary on the first day of the convention but oranges for fresh juice and mimosas for the new arrivals were a must. Other fruits for the rooms, cheeses for tea time. She'd need to do some baking. She checked the refrigerator. Cream, of course. Champagne? The wine cooler held several bottles, so she scratched it off the list.

Ginger's head snapped up and she stared out the kitchen window. *Ask Chink?* Those were the words scribbled in the corner of the marked up, scratched through, sheet of paper in Annette's room. She ran upstairs and threw open the door to the Bird Cage, then remembered. She had thrown it in the trash.

The maid's cart was stashed in the large utility closet on the second floor. Ginger tossed the ruined seat cushion to the floor and found what she was looking for. The old, yellowed sheet of notebook paper lay on top of the waste bin. She retrieved it and looked at it closely. If this was what she thought it was, then she was on the trail of a real treasure and perhaps the key to the mystery of Liberty's death. The question was, how did one fit with the other?

She debated about whether or not to call Duncan and decided against it. He was already annoyed with her for interfering in the case. There was nothing to show that Liberty's death was anything other than an overdose of alcohol and GHB. No one was going to kill her over her investigation into the welfare of the Hemingway cats. To Ginger's knowledge, Duncan hadn't yet found a relative of any kind to claim her body. The truth was, no one cared enough about Liberty one way or the other to kill her. Unless, of course, she was involved in whatever brought Annette to Key West.

Ginger took the piece of paper to the window of the Bird Cage and looked at it in the bright light. What she needed to do was determine what she had. She went downstairs to her quarters and booted up her laptop.

* * *

Sawyer couldn't be induced to reveal any more information about his business with Annette, but Trout didn't really need for him to do so. The nature of the object he was pursuing had been established regardless of what the actual prize might be.

He left the marina office and turned to retrace his steps back to the Paradise. Out of the corner of his eye he caught a glimpse of a silhouette. Someone had been standing among the roots of a banyan tree and when Trout passed by on the other side of the street, that someone moved. It was the way he moved that triggered the memory of the intruder for Trout.

The moment Trout turned and zeroed in on the slender figure, he broke and ran, proof positive that whoever he was, he had been either tailing Trout or spying on Sawyer. This time Trout had the advantage. This part of Key West was Trout's home base. The intruder wouldn't lose him again.

Trout anticipated the right turn onto Love Lane. The smaller streets offered better opportunity for his culprit to slip through residential areas and disappear. A car backed from an almost hidden driveway and blocked the runner. This caused the runner to check his pace and gave Trout the small advantage he needed. Just as his target was about to outmaneuver him once again, Trout reached out and caught the back of his shirt. Quick he might be, but he was no match for Trout's strength. Trout held tight to the dark blue tee shirt as his prisoner squirmed and kicked.

In the scuffle, the runner's baseball cap fell off. "Stop it!" Trout said. "You're caught."

The face that turned to him in fear wasn't a man after all, but a woman. The revelation caught Trout off guard and for a split second he was speechless.

"Who are you?" he asked but he needed no reply to his question. The aroma of cigars permeated the air around them. This, then, was the menace who had wreaked so much havoc on the staff at the Paradise.

When she remained silent, he gathered the collar of her shirt more securely, and marched her in the direction of the Paradise.

With his free hand he fished his cell phone out of his pocket and called Ginger.

"Get in touch with Duncan," he told her. "Have him swing by the business of Geraldo Mechoso." His captive tried to break free at those words. "It's a cigar factory, unless I'm very much mistaken. He should be able to figure out where it's located. Have him bring Mechoso to the bed and breakfast. It's time we got some answers."

Chapter Fifteen

I admit to being caught off guard by the apprehension of our young prowler. She doesn't seem very villainous to me, but then looks can be deceiving.

Duncan and a very unhappy Geraldo Mechoso sit across the room from Trout and his prize catch. Ginger is pouring tea that is being ignored. Who can blame them? We're finally going to get to the heart of this matter.

Duncan clears his throat. "Who wants to start?"

When no one responds he says, "I don't have all day. We can always do this down at the station."

"What have you done, Evita?" *Mechoso asks.*

She makes no reply.

"I'll tell you what she's done," *Trout says.* "She sent two people to the hospital with major head injuries and poisoned a third."

"Evita! Tell me this isn't true." *Mechoso rose to his feet, his expression one of grief and disbelief.*

Duncan stands as well, ready to act as necessary.

"I didn't kill anyone," *the young woman called Evita says.* "I swear it. I was there but I didn't do anything to her." *Tears begin to trail down her face.* "Please, Papa, you have to believe me."

"I'm the one you have to convince," *Duncan says.* "Tell me what happened. Otherwise, I have no choice but to charge you with murder."

"Murder!" *Mechoso and Evita say in unison.*

Duncan allows the silence to lengthen until Evita drops her head and says, "I didn't do anything to her. I was in the bathroom. I hid behind the door when I heard the key turning in the lock."

I leap onto Evita's lap and her hands automatically begin to furrow through my rich, thick coat.

"Who was with her?" *Duncan asks.* "Did you see him?"

Evita looks bewildered and shakes her head. "No one. She was alone."

Trout follows my lead and asks, "What happened, Evita?" *in that quiet tone of his that draws people to confide in him.*

She looks at Trout, fear evident in every aspect of her being. "I don't know. The door opened and I could hear her fumbling at the door, trying to fit the key on the inside lock. I realized I'd been caught."

"How did you do it without her creating a fuss?" *Duncan asks.*

"I didn't do anything," *Evita wails.* "She was drunk, okay? Stumbling across the room. I could hear her. She went over to the window and closed it. I was panicking, trying to decide how I was going to get out of there."

"How did you get out?" *Ginger asks.*

Evita looks from Duncan to Ginger and finally her gaze comes to rest on her father. "I heard her drop something, then she coughed a couple of times." *She swallows and holds me to her chest.* "The room got very quiet. I waited. After a while, I couldn't stand it any longer, so I slipped from behind the door." *She looks up at Duncan.* "She was passed out on the bed."

"No one else was in the room?" *he asks.*

Evita shakes her head.

"What then?" *Trout wants to know.*

"I left."

"How?" *Duncan, Trout, and Ginger say in unison.*

"Through the second window."

All three of them look from one to the other. Duncan takes Evita by the arm and when she stands, I'm dumped onto the floor. He marches her out into the foyer and up the stairs. When we reach the Toucan Suite, Ginger unlocks the door.

"Show me," *Duncan says.*

Evita looks at everyone crowded into the room. She crosses to the other side, slips behind the wingback chair before the second window, and draws back the drapes. She then lowers the top panel of it. With her hands on the top of the lower panel, she lifts her body over and out, and looks back into the room at Duncan, Trout, Ginger, and Geraldo Mechoso. "Like that," *she says.*

Trout is the first to reach the window and examine it. "The sash is cut. It appears to be locked but without the tension of the pulley weights, it can't be secured."

Ginger examines the damage to the window mechanism. "This is an old cut. Why didn't I realize this before now?"

"Probably because this window isn't used. The chair placement creates a natural traffic pattern from the room onto the gallery through the other window. It could have been this way for years."

"How did you know you could get in and out this way?" *Duncan asks Evita as he opens the other window and steps out onto the gallery.*

"I didn't." *She gives a little shake of her head and a slight shrug.* "I thought I'd go through this window so that when she woke up, she wouldn't realize anyone had been in the room. The chair blocks it and who bothers to move a chair and check the lock?" *She looks from one to the other.* "Nobody."

"That still doesn't explain how you got into the room in the first place," *Duncan says.*

"Oh, that part was easy. No one was around so I used the entry card, got the key off the board, went upstairs and unlocked the door."

"How did you get an entry card?" *Ginger wants to know.*

"I stole it from the desk earlier in the day."

This doesn't make Ginger happy. In fact, she's looking rather dismayed. Trout moves to her side and places an arm around her shoulders. She's feeling guilty, I expect, about the lack of security that has allowed these events to unfold at the Paradise. Well, there's nothing for it but to learn from our mistakes. In time she'll realize that Liberty's death would have occurred regardless of her security measures.

Trout is staring out across the gallery, lost in thought, it would seem. "How did Liberty get into her room when she arrived?"

"I left the key in the lock. I was going…" *Evita looks at her father.* "I was going to be in and out in a hurry, but I couldn't find it. That's how she caught me off guard."

"So, you thought that since she was drunk, she wouldn't remember the key in the door when she woke the next morning."

"Exactly. That's why I needed the room to be locked

from the inside."

"How did you get off the gallery?" *Ginger asks.*

Geraldo Mechoso answers for her. "She's a world class gymnast." *The look of disappointment on his face is heartbreaking.*

"Out and over the railing," *Duncan says with a sigh and a shake of his head.*

"That means Liberty really did die of a dose of GHB that occurred at some point before she returned to the Paradise," *Ginger says.*

Duncan rolls his shoulders in a shrug. "The obvious answer is usually the right answer."

Yes. Our man Duncan is correct on this one. Maybe the laid-back attitude masks a deep one. An air of regret that hovers around him tells me he's 'in the picture', as they say, on the current status of Ginger and Trout's relationship as well. No, not a bad detective after all.

* * *

Ginger handed the old notebook page across the kitchen worktable to Duncan. He read it, turned it over and checked the back, then handed it to Trout.

"So?"

"That's what everyone is looking for."

"An old sheet of paper with a bunch of scribbling and scratch outs on it?"

"It's Hemingway's scribbling." Ginger took the bottle of tequila from the pantry and set up three shot glasses. "That's what it's supposed to be anyway." She sliced a lime.

"How do you know this?" Trout asked.

She looked over his shoulder at the page and pointed at the notation in the bottom left-hand corner. "*Ask Chink* and the question mark."

"Who's Chink?" Duncan wanted to know.

"He was a patient at a hospital in Milan where Hemingway was recuperating during World War One." She passed around the shots and lime. "They became friends."

"Why does this matter?" Trout asked.

"His character is Catherine, see there?" she pointed. "She's modeled after Agnes von Kurowsky, Hemingway's first love and his nurse while he was recuperating."

"I don't see that this means anything."

"Catherine is the main character in *A Farewell to Arms*. He used people from his life as the basis for many of his characters throughout his career. I think this sheet of paper is meant to represent an early draft of that manuscript or at least notes he was making in the early stages of the idea for the story."

"Where did you find this?" Trout asked.

"I picked it up from the floor under Annette's bed when we were cleaning the room. At the time I thought it was trash, so I threw it in the bin. Later, after you left, it suddenly dawned on me what it was. It was the notation about Chink that made me realize it."

"Could this be the real thing?" Duncan asked.

The three of them exchanged a look.

"It could be, I suppose. Certainly, a lot of people seem to think it is," Ginger said.

No one said anything into the silence then they all threw back their shots and bit into the lime wedges.

"What will happen to Evita, Duncan?" Trout asked.

"They'll book her on the charges of breaking and entering and assault. That will hold her until Mechoso posts bail, if the judge allows it."

"You mean she's going to jail?" Ginger asked.

Duncan spread his hands in exasperation. "What do you think happens to criminals, Ginger?"

"She's just a kid," Trout said.

"A kid who sent two people to the hospital and one to the morgue."

"You don't believe that," Trout said.

"Yeah, well it gives me leverage until she comes clean about why she was in that room. We won't know she's truly innocent of poisoning Liberty until we know if she was looking for this sheet of paper. Why would anyone think Liberty had it in the first place?"

"Because Evita thought Liberty was Annette Benoit," Trout answered. "Somehow Evita learned about a literary agent coming to town to auction a lost Hemingway manuscript to the highest bidder. She knew that it was a blonde woman and that the Toucan Suite had been reserved for her."

"How did you know about the room reservations?" Ginger asked.

"It's the only thing that makes sense. You said Liberty didn't want the Bird Cage. That tells me you had to have had that room on the books for her when she arrived, right?"

"Yes."

"Instead, she ends up in the suite you planned to put your foreign guest in, the one with the added amenity of more space and access to the gallery."

"Right," Ginger said. "But how would Evita know?"

"Is your computer system password protected?" Trout asked.

"Yes."

"Does the staff know what the password is?"

Ginger hesitated. "Yes."

"And would the password be bird of paradise?"

Ginger's face turned red. "All this is my fault."

"No, it isn't," Duncan said. "Liberty was drugged off the premises. That could have happened regardless of where she was staying. This isn't about you and the Paradise, it's about someone willing to kill for scribblings on a piece of paper."

"What I don't understand is how Evita knew about any of this. It's true Geraldo came to the bed and breakfast looking for Annette before her disappearance with a story line that they had an appointment. He seemed truly caught off guard when he discovered what Evita had been doing. Regardless, he's involved somehow," Trout said.

He stared out the kitchen window at the two Hemingway cats making their way across the lawn. "You should talk to Sawyer," He suggested to Duncan. "He knows more about this than he's willing to tell me. Maybe he'll feel more inclined to answer your questions."

* * *

The thought of young Evita languishing in jail has me feeling rather sad. This strange concern for humans is becoming a nuisance. Since hooking up with Dax, I've become a real softie. So much for the indifference of cats. The situation doesn't sit well with Trout either. Such an outcome must take him back to memories of his former life.

Oh, dear, I do believe I'm depressing myself. I think what I need is a cool, quiet spot to reflect on the happenings at the Paradise and let the little gray cells, as Poirot, would say, do what they do best.

I find the climb to the fire escape landing is well worth the effort. A nice breeze rustles the palm fronds and creates a delightful background noise against the intrusion of city life. I understand why it's a favorite of Megs and Bartholomew. Up here, you're removed from the daily drama.

As I sprawl in the shade of the bed and breakfast, I feel as if I'm adrift on the high seas, the shushing of the palm fronds nudging me to the edge of sleep. Perhaps just a little snooze, then. It was probably such a lazy, drowsy state as this that Megs dreamed up the notion of Annette being a spy and hiding things.

I sigh. That ease is suddenly gone. What is it about Megs' ramblings that has left me awake and alert? That it was a shared dream, of course. She and Bartholomew both said they saw her hiding things, red and black things. Not too large things and not too small things.

I scramble to my feet and look into the window. Where could they witness something being hidden? There is only the view of the long hallway. A door near the other end opens into the Bird Cage. Next to that is the door to—oh, what silly name does Ginger call that guest room? The Blue Heron? That's it! Last is the door to the linen closet, right here, just inside the window.

* * *

Ginger looked up from sifting flour into a bowl when Callahan came dashing through the back door and slid to a stop at her feet.

"Yeow!"

"Not now, Callahan, I have my hands full."

"Yeow! Yeow!"

He trotted to the doorway that led from the kitchen into the dining room. When Ginger didn't stop what she was doing and follow after him, he came back, stood on his hind legs, and caught her apron with his claws.

"Seriously?" Ginger dusted the flour from her hands and disengaged his claws. "What is the matter with you?"

He twined between her legs, complaining all the while.

Ginger sighed, removed her apron, and followed after him. He was already at the top of the stairs before she could get to the foyer.

Trout looked up from the brochures he was organizing on an entryway table when Ginger strode across the foyer. "Where's the fire?"

"Apparently it's upstairs."

Trout fell in behind Ginger and they followed Callahan up the stairs, around the landing and to the back hallway. When they turned the corner, he was sitting in front of the linen closet.

"Oh, for pity's sake," Ginger said. "I think he's gone completely bonkers. This obsession with closed doors is going to be the death of me."

"Yeow!" Callahan stretched up and clawed at the doorknob of the linen closet.

"You're not getting in there and get cat hair all over my clean linens," Ginger said, as she marched down the hallway and caught Callahan up in her arms. "I have enough work to do without having to rewash all the sheets and towels."

Callahan squirmed from her grasp and began clawing in earnest at the door.

"He seems to be after something," Trout said.

"If you're implying I have mice, I'm going to knock your lights out, Trout." She tried to capture Callahan but he evaded her grasp. "That's the last thing I need with a house full of guests arriving the day after tomorrow."

Trout reached past her and opened the door to the

linen closet.

"Trout!" Ginger wailed.

Callahan dashed into the enclosure and began pawing among the stacks of sheets and towels.

"Great," Ginger muttered.

"Sorry, Ginger," Trout said, "but I think there's something more going on here than him being contrary and obsessed with closed doors." Trout began taking the sheets out of the closet and stacking them on the floor of the hallway.

When he lifted a stack of towels from the third shelf from the bottom of the closet, a black leather case trimmed in red fell to the floor.

"What in the heck?" Ginger asked, picking it up.

Callahan sat back on his haunches and said, "Yeow."

"This is what he wanted us to find," Trout said.

"But how..."

Trout looked at the cat, shook his head, and turned to Ginger. "Don't even go there."

* * *

The case sat in the middle of the kitchen worktable. Trout and Ginger stared at it. They had tried to open it but it was locked. After a while Ginger said, "We should call Duncan."

"In a bit," Trout said.

"You think this is what everyone is looking for, don't you?"

"Unless the Paradise has become the exchange point for political espionage. Have you had any James Bond lookalikes stay here lately?"

"You should write a book."

"Ha, ha."

"So, what should we do?" Ginger asked.

"I think it's time we made everyone show their hands."

"What do you mean?"

"We should round up all the usual suspects and see what they have to say about the mysterious locked case."

"Duncan won't like it."

"Probably not."

"It could be dangerous."

"Yes. It could."

They stared at the case. "Okay," Ginger said.

"Okay?"

"Yeah, okay." She took out her cell phone. "I'll look up Mr. Mechoso's number. Then I'll call the Curry Mansion Inn for Mr. Fortesque. You get Sawyer here."

"Four o'clock?"

Ginger nodded. "Four o'clock."

Chapter Sixteen

Well done, Trout. There's no need to let Duncan in on our little find just yet. Trout's idea to rattle the cage of all the contenders is what we need to find out what's really at stake here. I'm impressed that Ginger is willing to go along with the ploy.

The two of them might turn out to be decent detectives after all. That overriding desire to crack the case is like catnip. Or whatever humans crave. In this case I think it might be tequila. Nasty stuff if you ask me. How anyone could willingly drink something with a worm embalmed in it, I'll never know. As they say, to each his own.

What's this? I do believe the thrill of the chase has made Ginger a bit frisky. Enough of that, we still have a mystery to solve.

* * *

At a quarter to four Ginger was anxiously watching for the first arrivals. Instead of one of the three she was expecting, however, a dark, unmarked sedan pulled into the parking bay of the Paradise. She groaned inwardly. Duncan was about to spoil everything.

Instead of heading directly to the front steps of the bed and breakfast, he turned and opened the back door of the unmarked police car. Ray Talent emerged, followed by Crissy.

"Trout," Ginger called, "we have company."

Trout appeared from the hallway and when he saw Duncan marching the Talents up the steps of the Paradise, he swore under his breath.

"We'll have to tell him."

"I guess we will."

"Ginger," Duncan said as he entered the foyer.

"Looks like you've been busy," she said.

Duncan rolled his shoulders. "It occurred to me that I don't really have anything to charge these two with, unless, of course, they confess to breaking and entering. But, wait. They can't be charged with B and E, if they're paying guests. That and the fact that we don't know for sure that they actually did anything wrong."

Duncan looked hot and tired. Ginger realized the last few days had been a trial for him just as much as they had for her. His pride was also a little dented.

"I'm glad you came, Duncan," Ginger said and licked her lips. "The thing is, Trout and I found this case…"

The Talents looked at each other, then back at Ginger. Duncan looked like he would bite.

"I think it's what everyone is searching for." Ginger glanced from Ray to Crissy Talent. "But we wanted to be sure."

Duncan turned his glare on Trout. "Let me guess," he said. "You didn't call it in because you wanted to open it first. You wanted to make sure it was *significant* to the case." He heaved a soul-deep sigh. "The fact that there is no definitive crime being beside the point."

"Annette is still missing." Trout said.

"I spoke with Ms. Benoit's assistant. He isn't concerned about her whereabouts."

"Did he tell you why she was in Key West?"

"Business and a little pleasure was his answer to that question. When I inquired if he had heard from her, he said now and then, but couldn't say that he'd spoken to her within the last forty-eight hours."

"And that doesn't bother him?"

"No."

"It would bother me," Ginger said.

"Well, you're not French, are you? Apparently, her assistant has better things to do than be bothered with a nuisance visit from *l'officier de police*. It seems that in the absence of his employer, he doesn't feel the need to answer the phone, so when they came pounding on his door, he flushed all the good stuff."

"Really?"

Duncan threw up his hands in exasperation. "I don't know, Ginger! All I can tell you is that a visit from the police pissed him off and he's not in the least bit worried about Annette."

"Sorry, Duncan."

"Well, I had to call, regardless. Key West doesn't need an international incident involving a tourist." He held his finger in the air, closed his eyes, and when he opened them said, "It's been a long day. So, tell me about this case you found. Where was it?"

Trout glanced from Ray to Crissy and said, "Maybe we should hear what the Talents have to say about their involvement with Liberty Anderson."

Duncan angled his head in acquiescence and gestured toward the sitting room. Everyone trooped in and sat down except for Duncan. "Ask away," he said.

"Why were you following Ms. Anderson?" Ginger asked.

Ray and Crissy exchanged looks then he cleared his throat. "We didn't do anything wrong, okay? Mr. Fortesque just wanted us to follow her, see who she made contact with, let him know if … if anything changed hands with such contacts."

"By *anything* you mean…" Trout asked.

Ray shrugged. "Anything."

"Did you search her room?" Ginger asked.

Another quick glance at his wife, then he said, "No. That would be illegal."

Crissy sat forward and spoke in a nasal twang that reminded Ginger why they used Nashville as their address. "She was supposed to be the other one. The other blonde. But we didn't know that." She glanced at her husband. "She was supposed to be in the room next to us. The other one, that is. With the accent." She paused then used her index finger to point for emphasis, "But we didn't know she talked like that. How could we?"

"You didn't take anything from Ms. Anderson's room?" Duncan asked.

The Talents shook their heads.

"Did you ever enter the room?"

They looked at each other, then shook their heads again.

"Did you see anyone else enter Ms. Anderson's room?"

Again, the negative shake of the head.

"Why didn't you come back to the Paradise Saturday night?"

Ray said, "Mr. Fortesque paid us and said the job was done."

Duncan looked from Ginger to Trout, his eyebrows raised. "Any more questions?"

"No," Ginger said.

Trout shook his head.

"Get lost," Duncan said to the Talents.

"How are we supposed to get home?" Ray asked.

"Take a taxi with all that money Fortesque paid you," Duncan barked.

* * *

The Talents had just reached the sidewalk on Petronia in front of the Paradise Bed and Breakfast when Mr. Mechoso disembarked from a taxi. He gave them a glance in passing and came on up the walkway.

"He bailed out his daughter just a while ago so you can quit worrying on that score," Duncan said.

"Did you learn anything more from her at the station?" Trout asked.

"Not really. I can't figure out how she knew about it, whatever *it* really is, and why she would try to steal it."

"Sawyer told me something interesting about her grandfather."

"That he was buddy-buddy with Hemingway? Everyone knows that. I doubt there's an ounce of truth to it except both Geraldo Mechoso's father and Hemingway were in Cuba at the same time. The old man used to hang out at Sloppy Joe's telling his tall tales. After a time, no one really listened anymore."

When Mechoso walked through the front door into the foyer, he hesitated at the sight of Duncan.

"Don't worry, Mr. Mechoso," Duncan said, "I'm just here for the show."

Ginger came walking in from the dining room carrying the black leather case with red trimming.

"That's it, huh?" Duncan said.

"Do you recognize this, Mr. Mechoso," Trout asked.

He shook his head. "No. Should I?"

"This belongs to Annette Benoit, we believe."

"I see," he replied. "Have you looked inside?"

"Not yet," Ginger said. "We thought it would be better if we waited until all the interested parties were present."

"Who are all the parties?" he asked as the door behind him opened and everyone turned to see Sawyer enter the foyer.

"Geraldo," Sawyer said.

"Sawyer," Mechoso greeted him in return.

"I didn't know you were involved in this."

Mechoso said, "I'm not sure what *this* is."

Sawyer chuckled. "None of us are."

"Why did you come looking for Ms. Benoit, Mr. Mechoso?" Trout asked.

"She called me several weeks ago. She was looking for my father. When I told her he died five years ago, she asked if I still had the Hemingway letters."

"And?" Duncan asked.

"I told her yes, those and a photograph of Papa Hemingway with Bumby on a wooden horse my father had made for him. It was a letter of thanks for the gift to the boy. The picture was taken in the garden at *Finca Vigia* in Cuba." He pronounced the word coo-ba, as native Cubans do.

"What was her interest in them?" Ginger wanted to know.

"She said she thought she had a sample of his writing. Hemingway's writing. She wanted to compare it to something from that time in his life, to be sure. She also wanted to hear my father's stories."

"There was no offer to buy your letters?"

Mechoso shook his head. "No. She said she'd like to visit with me when she came to Key West, that she would be staying at the Paradise. There was a message on the telephone two days before I came here. She wanted to set an appointment but when I returned her call, she never answered. I left a message but when I didn't hear from her, I decided she had changed her mind."

"Why did you come to the Paradise then?" Trout asked.

"I wanted to see the paper. I wanted to see the handwriting and know that it looked like my father's letters."

"Validation of your father's stories," Trout said.

Mechoso made no reply.

"The phone message, that's how Evita knew about Annette and why she was here, isn't it?" Trout asked.

Mechoso glanced at Duncan but remained silent.

"She wanted the same thing. To honor her grandfather and make people realize he was a truthful man. If the handwriting matched, it would prove to the world that he had known the great Hemingway. That they had been friends." Trout spoke in that voice that reached through the pain and self-doubt.

Mechoso turned away and moved to the bay window in the sitting room. He stood there with his back to them all and stared out into the afternoon shadows.

Into the silence stepped Heronimous Fortesque, slightly breathless from the exertion of climbing the porch steps. His gaze flicked over the black and red case Ginger held in her hands. He smiled all around, his attention lingering on Duncan for a second longer than the rest.

"My, my, what have we here?" he asked.

"These are your fellow treasure hunters, Mr. Fortesque," Trout said, "and this, we believe, is the treasure." He nodded toward the case. "Shall we move into the sitting room since everyone is here?"

"And where is Ms. Benoit?" he asked as he settled himself on the love seat.

"Not here at the present," Trout said.

"Will she be joining us?"

"We hope so, but right now we're interested in what happened to Liberty Anderson."

"That again?" Fortesque said. "I told you she wasn't involved in the matter. The bumbling duo did follow her for a couple of days at my behest before they realized they had the wrong woman."

"Why would you hire someone to follow Ms. Benoit?" Duncan asked.

"Who're you?" Fortesque wanted to know.

"Detective Moore, Key West Police, currently looking into the circumstances surrounding Mrs. Anderson's death and Ms. Benoit's disappearance."

"Ms. Benoit is missing? What about the Hemingway papers? How can we conduct business if she's missing?"

"Your concern is touching," Duncan said.

"So, this is a gathering of the *usual suspects*, is it?" Fortesque laughed. "You, Detective Moore are no Louis Renault, and you," he inclined his head toward Trout, "are certainly no Humphrey Bogart." With a wave of his hand he said, "Please. Proceed. Tell us what any of us has to gain by Mrs. Anderson's death or Ms. Benoit's disappearance."

Ginger leaned in close to Trout and said in a low voice. "It worked so much better in the movies."

Sawyer spoke up. "Can we at least see what's in the case? Fortesque is right. No one here had any reason to harm either of those women. We all very much want Ms. Benoit to be alive and well and ready to pull a rabbit out of the hat."

Ginger placed the case on the coffee table. "It's locked," she said, "and we don't have the combination."

Sawyer slapped his hand against his forehead, Fortesque groaned and sat back on the love seat, Mechoso came to stand over the case. After a few seconds he asked, "Did you try Hemingway's birthday? It's a four-digit lock. Start with the year, eighteen ninety-nine."

Ginger knelt beside the coffee table and tried the numbers. She looked up at Mechoso and shook her head.

"July twenty-first doesn't lend itself to the correct number of digits. Maybe zero-seven-two-one."

Those numbers didn't work either.

"This is probably a case she's had for years and the code could be any number significant to her life. This is a gross waste of time," Duncan said. "We'll never figure out the combination."

"And why would you?" said a heavily accented woman's voice.

Everyone turned to see Annette Benoit standing in the entry into the sitting room with Jerry, the bartender from the Green Parrot, at her side. She was wearing an oversized man's tee shirt with a man's belt wrapped twice around her waist. She was very much alive and she looked fabulous.

* * *

Well, now, this is a sleight of hand I hadn't foreseen. Where, I wonder, has the lovely Annette been for the past two days? Pray one of these men can lift their chins off the floor to ask.

Duncan is the first to recover. A ladies' man usually is nimble with his reactions.

"Ms. Benoit," *he says with a certain something in his voice,* "I'm Duncan Moore with the Key West Police and we've been concerned about you."

"I remember you," *she says.*

"Well, it wasn't under the best of circumstances. That's why Ginger contacted me when you didn't return to your room for two nights."

"Why should I?" *she asks.* "This house is not safe. At every turn, people are being knocked in the head or dead. A man was in my room." *She is warming to the injustice of it all.* "In my locked room."

"We've caught the trespasser," *Moore says.*

"Oh." *His comment takes some of the wind out of her sails.* "Well, still, I couldn't think about sleeping here after what happened."

"Where have you been?" *Ginger asks.*

I glance at Jerry, the bartender from the Green Parrot and know the answer. Ginger is sweet and for someone who has seen a lot of life, a little naïve.

The straightforwardness of the Aussies comes out in full when Jerry *says,* "She's been staying with me."

Never mind chivalry, then. But at least my suspicions are confirmed.

"It would have been nice to know," *Ginger says with a touch of frost in her voice.*

Annette turns to Ginger with a look that beautiful women reserve for all other women. "I did not think of it. Why would you worry about me?"

Why, indeed? Or maybe it's just that she's French.

Never mind all that, it's time we got to the contents of the case. This has been at the heart of all the turmoil at the Paradise and I, for one, won't rest until I know what has caused all this grief for Ginger.

Trout appears to be in agreement with me.

"This is your case, Ms. Benoit?" *he asks.*

She flicks her head, sending her blond curls swinging back from her face. "Yes. This is my case. You had no right to try to open it."

"It's abandoned property," *Ginger says.* "It wasn't in your room. There's no identification on it. How could I begin to guess at ownership?"

Score one for Ginger. That red hair isn't wasted on her.

Annette once again focuses her attention on Ginger. You can see that she realizes she has misjudged the proprietress of the Paradise. She draws herself up to a new level of haughtiness and says, "I know the combination to the lock."

"Prove it," *Trout says.*

Annette lets her gaze travel around the room full of people. "Why should I? I don't know who these people are. The contents are very valuable and private."

"Is that why you hid them in the linen closet?" *Ginger asks.* "A very public place where all the staff of the Paradise might find them?"

"It was to be only for a day or two," *Annette says.* "The rooms were all empty except for the couple in the front. I didn't see the staff needing enough fresh towels to get to the level where the case was hidden." *She looks to Duncan in appeal.* "I knew someone was searching for it. That's why that man was in my room."

Apparently, Duncan has gotten a handle on himself. He says, "You still have to prove it's your case. The only way I know you can do that is to open it."

Annette is silent. I can almost see the wheels turning. How to get what she wants without giving anything.

Finally, she says, "Introduce me to all these men."

H. Fortesque steps forward, takes her hand, places a kiss on the back of it, and smiles. "Surely you remember me, Ms. Benoit."

She returns his smile. "Of course, Mr. Fortesque."

Mechoso nods his head, almost a bow. "I'm Geraldo Mechoso. We spoke on the phone about my father's letters."

"Yes," *Annette says,* "so kind you were to take my call."

That left Sawyer. He stands back from the others, biding his time. The mark of a man accustomed to getting his way, though you would not think it from his appearance. He's playing the long game.

Annette comes to him. She extends her hand, and he takes it but doesn't follow Fortesque's example. He merely holds it.

"Mr. Sawyer Daniels, I presume," *she says.*

"Ms. Benoit."

Annette steps back and lets her gaze travel over all of them before settling on Duncan. "I will open it, but only with a select few present." *She angles her head toward Duncan.* "You, of course, as a representative of the local authority. But only to see that I know the combination and the case is truly my possession."

"And?" *Duncan asks.*

"Mr. Fortesque and Mr. Daniels." *She pauses,* "And Mr. Mechoso."

Duncan glances to Ginger then Trout. He nods his head to Annette. "Deal."

Ginger starts to protest, and he says, "You want to get to the end of this or not?"

With a sigh, Ginger crosses her arms and nods.

Duncan herds everyone out of the sitting room except the precious few Annette has designated. And, of course, me. He closes the double doors.

* * *

Jerry looked from Ginger to Trout and said, "What's this all about?"

"It's a long story, Jerry." Trout could feel Ginger's annoyance. He wasn't real pleased himself at being booted from the great reveal.

"Well," Jerry said, "it was a good time while it lasted. I'd best be moving on. I'm on the clock at five."

"Right," Trout said.

Ginger seemed to rouse from her funk. "Jerry, thanks. For spreading the word about the Paradise."

"You bet." He turned toward the front door and stopped. "You know that woman you were asking about? The dead one?"

Trout perked up. "Yeah?"

"I could have sworn I saw her on the way over here today. Well, an older version of her, anyway."

"Mel," Trout and Ginger said in unison.

"Yeah, well, it kind of gave me that feeling, you know?

Like someone walking on your grave."

"She's not a ghost, Jerry," Trout said. "She'll move on as soon as she cuts through the red tape about her husband's ashes."

"That's supposed to reassure me?" Jerry asked.

Both Trout and Ginger laughed.

"It sounds spookier than it is, really."

"If you say so. Anyway, catch you later." With that, Jerry crossed the foyer and out the door just as Duncan appeared from the sitting room, closing the double doors behind him.

"So?" Ginger asked.

"It's hers. At least she knew the combination and that's good enough for me."

When he said nothing further, Ginger prompted, "Well?"

"Well, nothing. It has several file folders in it." Before Ginger could ask anything else, he raised his hand to silence her. "She wouldn't take anything out of the case while I was in there. For the eyes of her clientele only, she said."

"Duncan!" Ginger cried.

"Sorry, Ginger. She's within her rights, short of a suspicion of terrorist materials or drugs, to keep her business private."

Trout watched Mechoso through the glass panes of the double doors. He had donned a pair of white gloves and held a yellowed sheet of paper with reverence. Regardless of the authenticity of the papers, Trout felt they had accomplished at least one good thing.

"About Evita," Trout said.

Duncan rolled his shoulders. "It's been a long few days, Trout. Why don't we let that rest until we all have clearer heads. She's out on bail, safe at home with her parents. That's good enough for now."

"You can't charge her, Duncan," Ginger said.

"I already have, Ginger," he replied, a note of aggrievement in his voice.

"She's a young girl. Think what this will do to her life going forward." Ginger hesitated. "Besides, I won't press charges and neither will Jules."

"At this point, it isn't up to you."

"I won't testify against her."

Trout touched Ginger's elbow. "Tomorrow, Ginger," he said. "Duncan's right. We all could use a good night's sleep."

Duncan watched the interaction between Trout and Ginger and turned to look out the beveled glass door of the Paradise. "What made you look in the linen closet for the case?"

Trout and Ginger exchanged a glance.

"We were making up the rooms," Trout said. "Clean sheets, towels."

"We found it by accident," Ginger said.

"You on the payroll of the Paradise now?" Duncan asked Trout.

"Just helping out," he said.

"Uh huh." Duncan looked back at Trout and Ginger, a shadow of doubt in his eyes. "Well, if you quit your day job, you might make a halfway decent detective."

"Except we never did find out why Liberty was murdered."

"Just an unfortunate coincidence," Duncan said. "A soon-to-be divorcee in paradise looking to have a good time ended up the victim of a would-be rapist. End of story."

"I guess you're right," Trout said as he jangled the change in his pocket.

"I'm closing the books on this one," Duncan said, "and taking a few days of well-deserved time off. I don't want to hear another peep about goings on at the Paradise."

"Then you'd be well-advised to let Mel have Arty's ashes. She's like a bull terrier and I don't think you'll get any peace until she has them."

"What are you talking about?" Duncan asked.

"The ashes. From the Toucan suite. You know, Liberty Anderson's box of her dead husband's ashes."

"The other wife," Duncan said.

"The ex-wife," Ginger corrected him.

"She already has them," Duncan said.

"Since when?" Trout asked.

"Since, I don't know, the night she hit town."

Trout and Ginger looked at each other.

* * *

"Something isn't right," Ginger said to Trout as they watched Duncan walk down the steps of the Paradise and get into his car.

"And I think I know what it is," Trout said.

Ginger looked at him. "Why is she still in town?"

"Exactly," Trout said. "Especially since she's made such a stink about the cost of staying in Key West."

They turned in unison toward the stairs. In the open doorway of the Toucan Suite, they let their gazes travel around the room. What was it that kept Melissa Anderson in town long after there wasn't any need? What was it she sought? Ginger thought she knew. The only question was, where would Liberty have hidden it?

"The safe," Ginger said.

Trout opened the armoire to find the door of the safe standing open. "Too obvious. Let's start with the bed," he said.

They stripped the four-poster bed of the linens, checking thoroughly within the folds as they went. There was nothing under the mattress and Ginger shimmied under the bed to get a good look at the underside. No luck there.

All the drawers of the dressing table and highboy were removed and checked. Behind the armoire proved to be a dead end.

Hot and tired, Ginger sat back on her heels. "Where would she hide it?" she asked into the silence.

The sound of voices below and the closing of the front door gave notice that the party sequestered in the sitting room had broken up. Callahan came wandering into the room, an inquisitive look on his face.

Ginger scratched between his ears when he came to sit in front of her. "Where is it, huh?" she asked the cat.

He looked up at her and blinked, then sat gazing out the tall window.

Trout sat on the edge of the mattress and asked, "Where would you hide something that the average person wouldn't think to look? Something so out of the norm that even the cleaning staff wouldn't be a risk?"

Ginger shrugged. "We've checked beneath all the drawers for an envelope taped underneath. All the furniture, even the rug." She shook her head. "Where else is there? She must have done the same thing Annette did. It has to be hidden somewhere else in the Paradise."

Trout didn't respond and he didn't move. His gaze was fixed on the middle distance, lost in thought.

Callahan jumped onto the shelf in a recess of the room between the front wall and the enclosed duct space for the air conditioner venting. It served as a small work space, and in the corner was a coffee pot for guests to have a fresh cup while they prepared for their day. He sniffed at the little basket containing condiments.

Ginger watched him and suddenly inhaled sharply. "The microwave."

Trout stood.

"In the cabinet below the television," she said.

He opened the cabinet, then the door to the microwave. It was empty.

"Well, it was a thought," Ginger said, disappointment in her voice.

"We need to undo all this havoc," Trout said. He adjusted the mattress with a push of his knee and pulled a sheet from the pile of linens they had taken from the bed.

It took them twice as long to restore everything to order as it had for them to wreck it. They stood in the middle of the room and eyed their handiwork. "That was a wild goose chase," Ginger said.

"We could be wrong," Trout said.

They looked at each other and shook their heads.

"Where to look, then?" he asked.

"I haven't the foggiest."

"We're done here, I guess," Trout said as he pushed the bathroom door wide and glanced inside. The cat was sitting on the closed toilet.

"Yeow."

"I've already checked in here," he said to the cat. "But

it was a good thought."

"Are you talking to the cat?" Ginger asked with a smile.

"I suppose I am."

"There's no place to hide anything in the bathroom. We've checked the cabinet beneath the sink and the medicine chest. Let's call this room a wrap." She motioned toward the cat. "Come on Callahan. This room is ready for guests and I don't want to have to revisit it with the vacuum chasing cat hair."

"Yeow," he said and remained where he sat.

Ginger and Trout watched the cat who in turn watched them. She let her gaze travel around the room until it came to rest on the stack of snowy white towels on the shelf above the toilet.

The a-ha moment was like a chilled finger running down her spine. She crossed the bathroom and began shaking out the towels. On the third one in the pile, a blue legal document fell to the tiled floor.

"The will," Ginger and Trout said in unison.

Chapter Seventeen

I confess to having been fooled by Mel Anderson. I'm a big enough cat to acknowledge that her aggressiveness toward Liberty was the perfect foil to any inquiries about her story. Lesson learned. In the future I'll remember the old adage that in the case of murder, everyone's a suspect.

It was a good ploy and it worked for a while but like Trout and Ginger, I don't believe in coincidences. The resolution to the case didn't sit well with me or them and to their credit, they refused to let it go.

For all the skullduggery surrounding Annette Benoit and her found treasure, the true crime was the original one, the murder of Liberty Anderson. The motive was a classic one. Money. She as much as told us so when we first met her at the Paradise. Her ex-husband's beneficiary hadn't yet been settled. In the end, it was all about the inheritance of his estate.

I've watched enough Law and Order shows with my various human acquaintances to know the age-old truism. It's always the ex-wife.

If she hadn't hung around Key West in the hope of gaining access to the Paradise to search for the will, she might have gotten away with it.

Duncan has taken Mel into custody on the circumstantial evidence we now have. It's only a matter of time until all that dogged legwork, which is the headache of policing, bears fruit and someone will come forward with further information. Two women who looked so much alike can't have gone unnoticed by some local.

It's a lucky thing for Duncan that the search of Mel's residence has produced evidence that she "cooked" her own GHB. It will be a simple enough task for the forensics team to prove it's the same batch that was found in Liberty's system.

Mel's computer is in the hands of the police in D.C. My guess is that they will find that the complaint about the Hemingway cats was generated from her laptop. That was rather a clever touch by Mel, to move the crime scene from a location where suspicion would fall on her.

The guests for the convention arrived yesterday. Mimosas are free-flowing and everyone is in a jovial mood except for the crusty old bat in the Blue Heron. I may be in paradise but I wouldn't have Ginger's job for all the tea in China.

Trout is manning the tiki bar and Harry is fetching and carrying. Dax is enjoying a beer in a lounger under the newly erected awning over the freshly painted door of the garage apartment. Jules will return to work tomorrow and Ginger is happy. All is well in Paradise.

* * *

Trout watched Duncan stroll across the side lawn of

the Paradise to the tiki bar. "Duncan," he said by way of greeting, "you're looking rested."

The detective deposited himself on one of the bar stools. "It's amazing what a couple of nights' sleep will do," he replied. He looked around at the people reclining by the pool, laughing and having a good time. "Looks like it's business as usual."

"Pretty much."

Duncan watched Trout mix a drink and hand it off to Harry. "So, you give up the charter business or what?"

"No," Trout said. "Just helping out until Jules returns tomorrow."

"Huh." Duncan took a sip of the gin and tonic Trout placed before him. "How's Ginger?"

"I think she'll be fine. Still a little squeamish about Liberty dying on the premises but that will pass with time."

"Didn't seem to hurt her business."

"No. Sawyer was right about that. She's been getting a lot of calls for the Toucan Suite. Apparently, there are a lot of people who like the idea of a dead body in a locked room."

"How'd that get out, I wonder?"

"Beats me, but the Ghosts and Gravestones tour is already including it in their spiel like he said they would."

"Where is he anyway?" Duncan asked. "Haven't seen him since the great reveal."

Trout grinned. "On the *Big Buddha*. With Ms. Benoit."

Duncan laughed. "You don't say. Looks like they struck a deal. Was the article of interest genuine?"

"Who knows, but I think Sawyer will enjoy finding out."

* * *

Ginger checked on Jules at the front desk, straightened the tourist brochures and wandered out onto the porch. Trout was lounging on the swing reading *Old Possum's Book of Practical Cats*. He looked up when Ginger crossed to where he sat.

"Caught out," he said with a smile.

Ginger laughed. "Come on," she reached out her hand to him, "let's walk down to Mallory Pier and watch the sunset."

Trout took her hand, and they strolled south to the gathering point of tourists and conchs alike for mother nature's grand finale. Callahan trotted along at their heels.

There was a light breeze off the water and Trout stood behind Ginger, his arms around her as they faced west and waited. On a piling in front of them Callahan sat, also looking out across the water as the last of the sun turned the sky orange and red in a spectacular halo.

"What do you imagine he's thinking?" Trout asked Ginger.

"I believe he's contemplating his singular name," she replied.

Author's Note

A friend pointed out to me that I somehow manage to have an animal in most of my stories. It isn't something that I did consciously until I started writing about first Trouble, then Callahan. Maybe my spirit animal is a cat.

Thank you for taking the time to read *Callahan and the Spy*. If you enjoyed it, please consider telling your friends or posting a short review. Word of mouth is an author's best friend and is much appreciated.

Thank you!

Cat Callahan Mysteries by Rebecca Barrett and Susan Yawn Tanner:

Callahan on the Case
Callahan and the Horses of Hope
Callahan's Savannah Caper
Callahan Goes Rodeo
Callahan and the Spy
Callahan in Action

Callahan's Christmas Feast (short story)
A Callahan Christmas (short story)

An avid reader since the bookmobile began coming to their farm when she was a child, Rebecca Barrett now happily lives in the lovely village of Fairhope, Alabama, situated on Mobile Bay, where she finds inspiration all around her.

Visit her website at rebeccabarrett.com

She can be reached by email at:

barrett.author@gmail.com